NOW

Gm: Nina
Ella ∞ Sam
Robin Licia   Freddy ∞ Julie   Emma
                  Becky Joe

Also by Gabriel Josipovici

FICTION
The Inventory (1968)
Words (1971)
Mobius the Stripper: stories and short plays (1974)
The Present (1975)
Four Stories (1977)
Migrations (1977)
The Echo Chamber (1979)
The Air We Breathe (1981)
Conversations in Another Room (1984)
Contre-Jour: a triptych after Pierre Bonnard (1984)
In the Fertile Land (1987)
Steps: selected fiction and drama (1990)
The Big Glass (1991)
In a Hotel Garden (1993)
Moo Pak (1995)

THEATRE
Mobius the Stripper (1974)
Vergil Dying (1977)

NON-FICTION
The World and the Book (1971; 1979)
The Lessons of Modernism (1977; 1987)
Writing and the Body (1982)
The Mirror of Criticism: selected reviews (1983)
The Book of God: a response to the Bible (1988; 1990)
Text and Voice: essays 1981–1991 (1992)
(ed.) The Modern English Novel:
the reader, the writer and the book (1975)
(ed.) The Sirens' Song:
selected essays of Maurice Blanchot (1980)

GABRIEL JOSIPOVICI

Now

CARCANET

First published in Great Britain in 1998 by
Carcanet Press Limited
4th Floor, Conavon Court
12–16 Blackfriars Street
Manchester M3 5BQ

Copyright © Gabriel Josipovici 1998

The right of Gabriel Josipovici to be identified
as the author of this book has been asserted
by him in accordance with the Copyright,
Designs and Patents Act of 1988.
All rights reserved.

A CIP catalogue record for this book
is available from the British Library.

ISBN 1 85754 367 X

The publisher acknowledges financial
assistance from the Arts Council of England.

Set in Berling by SetSystems, Saffron Walden
Printed and bound in England by SRP Ltd, Exeter.

'So instead of getting to Heaven, at last –
I'm going, all along.'

Emily Dickinson

—I'm tired, Licia says.
—Nobody's tired at your age, Sam says.
—I'm tired.
—At my age you've got a right to be tired, Sam says. Not at your age.
—What has right to do with it?
—It's not natural.
—Leave her alone Dad, Freddy says.
—Nobody's tired at her age, Sam says. Are you tired?
—Sure.
—All the time?
—Most of the time.
—That's because you work too hard.
—No I don't, Freddy says.
—But what does she do? Sam says. I'll tell you what she does. She does nothing. That's why she's tired. That's why she thinks she's tired. If she got a job like everyone else she wouldn't have time to feel tired.
—Let it go Dad, Freddy says.
—The laburnum's in flower, Nina says.
—If you've got something to do you don't have time to feel tired, Sam says.
—I can see it from my window, Nina says. Quite suddenly, it's all in flower.
—If she hadn't given up her job she wouldn't feel so tired, Sam says.
—Let it go Dad, Freddy says.
—You can't see it from here, Nina says. But you can from my window.
—You've got a lovely view from your window, Julie says.
—I look right down on it, Nina says. If my arms were just a bit longer I could lean out and touch it.
—At least if you got up at a normal time you wouldn't feel so tired, Sam says to his daughter.
—I'm too tired to get up at a normal time, Licia says.

—That's what I'm telling you, Sam says. If you got up at a normal time you wouldn't feel so tired.

—Let it go Dad, Freddy says. Let it go.

—She says she's tired, Sam says. I tell her what to do to stop being tired. What's wrong with that?

—Soon the chestnuts will be in flower as well, Nina says. First the white and then the pink.

—What's wrong with that? Sam says to his wife.

—Nothing dear, Ella says.

—That's what I'm telling him, Sam says. You don't think I love her? he says to his son.

—Come on Dad.

—You don't think I do?

—Give us a break Dad.

—First the white, Nina says, and then the pink.

—Can you see them from your window? Julie asks her.

—See what dear?

—The chestnut trees.

—Oh yes, Nina says.

—That's nice, Julie says.

—In the winter of course I can see much further, Nina says. Because the trees are bare then.

—How far can you see?

—Right up to the Common.

—But then you don't have the window open.

—Only at night, Nina says. I always open the window at night. When I go to sleep. And turn the heating off. I always have, haven't I? she says to her daughter.

—Yes Mother, Ella says.

—Of course there wasn't any heating in the old days, Nina says. So you didn't have to turn it off.

Freddy looks at his watch.

—Some people had air-conditioning, Nina says. We never did. We didn't even think of it.

Freddy tries to catch his wife's eye. OK? he mouths at her.

She nods.

—As long as you didn't have to go out in the heat it was all right, Nina says. As long as you could keep everything shut in the daytime. To keep in the cool. To keep out the heat.

Freddy and Julie stand up.

—You don't have to go yet, Ella says to her son.

—Nowadays, Nina says, you always have to think about turning it off. In the winter, that is, when it's on.

—Tell him to stay a little longer, Ella says to her husband.
—Maybe he's got things to do, Sam says.
—Like what?
—How should I know?
—You've got things to do? Ella asks her son.
—That's why I don't like sleeping in hotels, Nina says. You can never turn off the heating at night.

Freddy kisses his mother.
—You're going already? she says.
—Sometimes, Nina says, you can't even find the thing. What's it called?

Freddy winks at his sister.
—What's it called? Nina says.
—What's what called?
—The thing that heats.
—A fire?
—No no.
—A stove?
—No no. You know . . . For the central . . . the central heating.
—You mean the boiler?
—Yes, that's it. No. Not the boiler. No.
—The radiator?
—That's it. The radiator.

Freddy puts a hand on his father's arm. —I'll call you, he says to his mother.
—Call you, call you? Nina says. Why can't people speak English any more? Why do they have to use these Americanisms all the time? In my day call meant shout, she says. Now it means telephone. It shouldn't be allowed.
—Why not? Licia says.
—Why not what?
—Why shouldn't it be allowed?
—Because she says so, her father says. Isn't that enough?
—So she decides?
—In my house she decides, Sam says. Isn't that so? he asks his wife.
—Yes dear, Ella says.

*

Julie fastens the seat-belt with one hand as she steers the car out into the road with the other.
—She's not senile, Freddy says. You don't have to humour her.
—I know she's not senile, Julie says.

—Then you don't have to humour her.
—Who's humouring her? Julie says, craning her neck at the crossroads.
—You were.
—Me?
—Oh come on! Freddy says.
—Come on what?
—I heard you, Freddy says.
—Heard me what?
—Humouring her.
—You heard me humouring her?
—You're not going to say you weren't?
—Of course I wasn't. We were having a perfectly reasonable conversation.
—You call that a perfectly reasonable conversation?
—Anything coming from the left?
—No.
—You call that a perfectly reasonable conversation? Freddy says again.
—Are you trying to tell me how to behave? Julie says.
—Of course not. You're the counsellor.
—What's that got to do with it?
—It means you're an expert in behaviour.
—You think it means that?
—What does it mean then?
—It doesn't mean anything, Julie says, opening up the roof. It's a job I do, that's all.
—All right, Freddy says. It doesn't mean anything. But there's no need to humour her.
—I wasn't humouring her.
—I heard you.
—Are you trying to tell me how to behave?
—It's embarrassing, Freddy says.
—Embarrassing? Who for?
—She doesn't need anyone to feed her questions. She's perfectly happy talking on her own.
—Now you're the one who's saying she's senile.
—I am?
—Aren't you?
—Not at all. I just stated a fact. She likes to talk but she doesn't need anyone to feed her questions.
—That's incredible, Julie says.
—What's incredible?

—What you've just said.

—It's incredible? What I've just said is incredible? Can you tell me why?

—It's just incredible. You should hear yourself.

—You should hear *your*self. Putting on that voice to speak to her.

—What voice?

—You know what voice.

Julie pulls in opposite the tube station. —What time will you be in? she asks.

—You don't hear the voice you have when you speak to her? he asks.

—I can't stop here, Julie says. What time will you be in?

—When I'm done.

—I'm supposed to tell that to the children?

—You want to start lying to them?

—I thought you might have forgotten you were reading to Joe tonight.

—Do I usually forget?

—There's always a first time.

—That's what you say to your patients?

—Clients.

—That's what you say to your clients?

—I can't stay here, she says. Are you getting out or not?

He opens the door of the car. —I won't forget, he says. I'm looking forward to it.

—You'd better not, she says.

—What does that mean?

—Come on, she says. Get out.

He slams the door and watches as she steers out into the traffic. —I'm looking forward to it! he shouts after her.

—Robin rang, Ella says to her daughter.
—Oh yes? Licia says.
—I told him you'd ring back.
—I told you not to say that.
—What else could I say?
—Nothing.
—I had to say something.
—You could say you'd pass on the message.
—He wanted to speak to you.
—He always wants to speak to me.
—You weren't there.
—That's right, Licia says.
—Did you go for a walk?
—Uhuh.
—Do you want a cup of tea?
—No thanks.
—You've had some?
—No.
—Then why not have a cup?
—I don't feel like it.
—Aren't you cold?
—No.
—Just a little call, Ella says. It's not very much to ask.
—But I don't want to speak to him.
—Why not?
—I don't like him.
—You don't like him?
—I've told you. I don't like him.
—What's wrong with him?
—Nothing.
—Then why don't you want to speak to him?
—Because I don't like him.
—Why?
—Why what?
—Why don't you like him?

—I just don't.
—I like him, Ella says.
—Then you speak to him.
—I spoke to him.
—Speak to him again. Ring him up and speak to him.
—It's not me he wants to speak to, Ella says. It's you.
—But I don't want to speak to him.
—Why not?
—I don't like him.
—What don't you like about him?
—Everything.
—Everything?
—I don't like him ringing up all the time.
—He wouldn't if you returned his calls.
—I don't want to speak to him. I don't like him. He gets on my nerves.
—You used to like him, Ella says.
—Never.
—Yes you did. Why did you go out with him?
—Mum, Licia says, I *tolerated* him. Now I don't. That's all.
—You're sure you won't have a cup of tea?
—No.
—I'm just making myself a cup.
—Go ahead.
—What shall I tell him if he rings again?
—Say you'll pass on the message.
—But there isn't any message. He just wants to speak to you.
—What about?
—He didn't say.
—He doesn't want to speak to me about anything, Licia says.
—He just wants to speak to you, Ella says.
—Just tell him you'll pass on the message.
—But then he'll ring up again.
—Tell him you've passed on the message.
—I can't do that. It's rude.
—It's rude to ring up all the time.
—He just wants to speak to you, Ella says.
—I know, Licia says.

*

—But what have I said? Freddy says. What have I said? Tell me what I've said.
—What have you said? Petra says. Oh come *on*! Come *on*!

—No, Freddy says. Just tell me. Tell me what I've said.
—Come *on*! Petra says.
He gets out of bed. He begins to dress.
—You said, she says, we've *had* the whole afternoon.
—Well we have, haven't we?
—The whole afternoon? Petra says. From four to six is the whole afternoon?
—Well what is it then? The whole morning?
—It's two hours, that's what it is, Petra says. Two hours. One hundred and twenty bloody minutes.
—One hundred and twenty minutes is a long time, Freddy says.
—What's that supposed to mean?
—Mean? It means it's a long time, he says, putting on his trousers.
—You know what that sounds like? she says.
—What?
—It sounds like with me every minute drags.
—I didn't say that.
—You implied it.
—I said it was the whole afternoon, he says, knotting his tie. In answer to your query about surely I wasn't about to go so soon. That's all I said.
—One of *your* afternoons, she says.
—One of *my* afternoons? What's that supposed to mean? he says.
—You don't even take your watch off in bed, she says.
—Passion overcame me, he says.
—Is that why you kept sneaking a look at it all the time?
—Oh come on, he says.
—Don't think I didn't notice.
—I have to think about the time, he says.
—Exactly, she says.
—I have to get to this show, he says.
—Why? she says.
—Because it's my job, he says. That's why.
—You could do it tomorrow, she says. It wouldn't make any difference.
He combs his hair in the mirror.
—You only have to have your piece in by Wednesday, she says.
He puts the comb back in his pocket and straightens his jacket.
—You just don't care, do you? she says.
—Look, he says, turning towards her, hands open in front of him. I . . .
—You could come back here afterwards, she says.
—I'm reading to Joe this evening.

8

—Why can't Julie?
—Because it's my turn.
—And it's never my turn?
He pockets his keys.
—I'm sorry, she says. She gets out of bed and pulls on a dressing-gown. —I'll make some coffee, she says.
—Thanks.
—I'm sorry, she says, holding him. I want to be with you so much.
—Me too, he says.
She stands on tiptoe and kisses him.
—What about that coffee? he says.

*

—Do you want some tea? Ella says to her husband. I've just made some.
—No thanks.
—No?
—No thanks.
He sits down at the kitchen table.
—Simon rang, she says. He wants you to fetch him next Sunday.
—Fetch him? Sam says. From where?
—He's sprained his ankle.
—He's what?
—He's sprained his ankle.
—He's sprained his ankle?
—That's what he said.
—Can't he take a taxi?
—He won't. You know what he's like.
—I'll pay.
—He wouldn't let you.
—Then let him take the tube.
—He can't. He's sprained his ankle. It's all swollen up.
—I'm not fetching him.
—He thought at first he'd broken his leg.
—I'm not fetching him.
—He could have broken it, she says. Or his hip.
—He should stay at home, he says. Keep warm.
—That's what he's doing.
—He needs to stay warm till the swelling goes down. Stay indoors for a week or two.
—He wants so much to come. He says he'd hate to miss a Sunday.
—I'm not fetching him.

—He can't stay at home all the time. He'll go crazy.
—He is crazy.
—You know it's not good for him.
—Of course it's good for him. It's what he needs. Moving must be agony.
—He says it's not too bad.
—Then he can hobble down to the tube.
—He can't do that. He can't put any weight on it. It's all right when the foot's up but he can't put any weight on it.
—That's what I'm saying, Sam says. He needs to stay at home and keep his leg up.
—He looks forward to his Sunday lunches, she says. He doesn't have much in his life.
—He shouldn't sprain his ankle then.
—He didn't do it on purpose.
—How do you know?
—Why should he do something like that on purpose?
—I'm not fetching him, Sam says. That's final. Either he gets here under his own steam or he stays at home.
—It won't take long on a Sunday, Ella says. The roads are empty.
—Empty? You must be joking.
—You're sure you don't want a cup of tea?
—Have you seen what the roads are like on Sundays these days?
—Or a biscuit?
—No thanks.
—It won't take long on a Sunday, she says.
—I've just told you, he says. The roads are even busier on Sundays than during the week nowadays. Everybody's rushing somewhere and as a result it takes twice as long to get anywhere.
—What shall I tell him then?
—Tell him what I've just said. Either he takes a taxi or he stays at home.
—He won't like it.
—And what about me? he says. Do you think I'll like spending my Sundays sitting in traffic jams and listening to your uncle jabbering on about himself?
—It's not as bad as that, she says.
—He's twice as bad, he says.
—He's an old man.
—So am I.
—You're not.
—I *feel* old.
—But he *is* old.

—He shouldn't have sprained his ankle.
—He didn't do it on purpose.
—How do you know?
—Who'd do something like that on purpose?
—Perhaps he wanted to annoy me.
—He doesn't want to annoy anyone. It's not in his nature.
—It isn't?
—Of course it isn't. You know him as well as I do.
—I wouldn't put it past him.
—Simon?
—Maybe it's fate, he says.
—What is?
—Maybe he's fated not to come here on Sunday.
—But he wants to come. It takes him out of himself.
—That's what fate is, he says. You want to do something but the gods rule otherwise. You want to be taken out of yourself but it's not to be.
—It could be if you fetched him.
—I'm not fetching him. Why doesn't he take the tube?
—He can't. His ankle's all swollen up.
—Perhaps it'll have gone down by Sunday.
—And if it hasn't?
—He can take a taxi. I'll pay.
—He wouldn't let you.
—Then let him pay.
—He can't afford it.
—Of course he can. He's just mean.
—He's never taken a taxi in his life.
—That's what I'm saying. He's a mean old man.
—He's just not extravagant, that's all.
—All right, he says. But I'm not fetching him.

—Personally, Steve says, I'd have liked more of the early stuff.
—Kate said they'd be concentrating on the Bauhaus years.
—Of course they are, Steve says. And you know why.
—Why?
—Because the Russians aren't letting any of the early stuff out.
—What have the Russians got to do with it?
—He wasn't French you know.
—How many Parisian artists were?
—True.
—You could count them on the thumbs of one hand.
—Two hands.
—All right. Two hands.
—Braque and Leger.
—I wanted to talk to you, Robin says to Freddy.
—Oh yes?
—Actually when you count up there's a fair number. Starting with Bonnard and Vuillard and if you include people like Corbusier and Michaux.
—What do you mean people like Corbusier and Michaux?
—Can we get out of this crush? Robin says.
—I don't know that we can, Freddy says. It's even worse next door.
—I mean people who weren't primarily artists.
—Well what were they if they weren't artists?
—I said primarily artists.
They squeeze out into the central hall.
—Yes? Freddy says.
—It's Licia, Robin says. She won't return my calls.
—Why not?
—I don't know.
—You didn't ask her?
—How can I if she doesn't return my calls?
—She's out a lot these days, Freddy says.
—Out? Where? I thought she'd thrown in her job?
—Just out.

—She's got another job?
—Not that I know.
—She gets your mother to answer the phone and say she's not there, Robin says.
—She's not, Freddy says.
—Where is she then?
—You'll have to ask her.
—I don't want to pester her, Robin says. I respect her privacy. I just wanted to find out how she was.
—She's fine, Freddy says.
—Fine? You mean she's fine?
—That's right.
—You're not worried about her?
—Worried?
—I just thought . . . You don't feel things are a bit difficult for her at the moment?
—Why?
—I just thought she . . .
—She what?
—I don't want to pester her, you understand, Robin says. But I just thought . . . Could you tell her if there's anything I can do . . .
—Anything like what?
—I don't know. Anything I can do. To help.
—To help?
—Anything at all . . .
—Buona sera, buona sera, Nigel says, materialising beside them.
—You seem very chirpy this evening, Freddy says.
—Do I? Why's it so crowded in here?
—Darling! a lady says, embracing Robin. How lovely to see you!
—I wanted to ask you, Nigel says to Freddy. The other day Benjy asked me if I'd be prepared to write the intro to the Nash show and I half agreed but now I've been approached by a publisher to –
—I'm sorry, Freddy says. I've got to get home.
—No but listen. I wonder if you'd be interested in –
—I'm late with three deadlines as it is, Freddy says.
—I just thought, given your interests –
—Just tell her to get in touch when she feels like it, will you? Robin says, pressing his arm.
—Sure.
—You won't forget?
—I'll tell her.
—Good man.
—They pay quite well, Nigel says.

—I'm sorry, Freddy says. I've got to get home.
—What's the rush?
—I'm reading to my little boy.
—Reading to him?
—Uhuh.
—What?
—What?
—What are you reading to him?
—What am I reading to him?
—Yes. What?
—Calvin's *Institutes*.
—Never heard of it. Is it good?
—'Bye, Freddy says.
At the entrance people are still pushing their way in.
—Why is it so crowded?
—It's the new policy.
—What new policy?
—Haven't you heard?
—You'd have thought they –
—They want to create the sense of something happening.
—Ronny's idea?
—Who else?
—Damn silly if no one can breathe, isn't it?
—You come to these things expecting to breathe? And what else? Un verre de champagne et une femme sur un canapé? as my French teacher used to say to us.
  —Well, here goes. Head down and elbows out.
  —Good luck.
  —Cheerio.

*

—Your mother rang, Julie says. She wants you to call her.
—Now?
—As soon as you got home, she said.
—All right.
—Don't be on the phone all night. Joe's waiting.
—It's me, he says to his mother.
—Where were you?
—Working.
—Working? At this time of night?
—It's my job.
—You work too hard.
—I know. What did you want?

—You looked tired at lunch. Couldn't you do a bit less?
—Was that what you rang about?
—No. It's about Uncle Simon.
—What about him?
—He's sprained his ankle.
—Sprained his ankle?
—Yes.
—How?
—Getting out of the bath. He could have broken his leg. Or his hip. But he only sprained his ankle.
—I'm sorry.
—Dad wondered if you'd fetch him on Sunday.
—Me?
—Yes.
—Why?
—He can't walk. His ankle's all swollen up.
—No. I mean why me?
—Dad says he won't do it.
—Quite right.
—He can't walk. His ankle's all swollen up. He can't put any weight on it.
—Can't he take a taxi?
—You know Uncle Simon never takes taxis.
—Maybe he could make an exception.
—He says if he starts making exceptions there'll be no end to it.
—I'm not fetching him.
—He's in terrible pain.
—Then the best thing is to stay at home.
—He says it'll do him good to get out.
—Then let him take a taxi. Dad'll pay.
—Uncle Simon won't let him.
—How do you know? Have you asked him?
—I know. He just wouldn't. He thinks it's sinful.
—Sinful? To take a taxi?
—To pay all that money.
—And it's not sinful to have someone come all the way out to fetch you and then have to take you all the way back?
—It's no trouble on Sundays. The roads are empty.
—Then what's the problem?
—Dad won't do it. He says the traffic's got worse recently on Sundays.
—He's right. It has.
—He thought you might.

—Might what?
—Fetch him.
—Sorry.
—You mean you won't?
—Yes.
—Then how's he going to get here?
—I don't know.
—He can't take a tube. Not with his ankle in that condition.
—Tell him to take a taxi.
—He won't do that.
—Then that's it, isn't it?
—I suppose so, dear.
—Why don't you put it to him that it's less sinful to take a taxi than have someone drive all the way out to fetch you?
—You think I should?
—Why not?
—I'll try.
—Do that, Mum.
—He won't like it.
—Then he stays at home.
—He looks forward to his Sundays with us.
—Then let him find his own way.
—I'll try, she says. But I know he won't like it.
—I'm sorry, Freddy says as he enters the bedroom. I was on the phone to Granny. Uncle Simon's sprained his ankle.
—Playing football?
—Football? Uncle Simon?
—Why not? There's a really old man who plays in the park.
—Not as old as Uncle Simon.
—Yes. Really old. With a white beard.
—I don't think Uncle Simon's ever kicked a ball in his life.
—How did he do it then?
—He fell getting out of the bath.
—I didn't think Uncle Simon ever took a bath.
—You mean because he smells?
—Yes.
—Well it seems he does.
—Is it all swollen up?
—Yes.
—He should put an ice-pack on it.
—You should tell him.
—A pack of frozen peas will do.
—How do you know?

—Everyone knows that.
—Do you want to hear a story?
—Yes.
—All right. Relax. Close your eyes.
—They are closed.
—No they're not.
—Now they are.
—Right. 'Once upon a time there was a fisherman and his wife who lived together in a stinking hovel on the shore of the sea, and every day the fisherman—'
—What's a hovel?
—A tumbledown hut.
—What's tumbledown?
—Falling to pieces. Can I go on?
—Yes.
—'And every day the fisherman would go out and fish. And he fished and fished. And one day he was sitting there with his line and looking into the clear water. And he sat and sat. And then his line went right down to the bottom and when he drew it up there was a big flounder on the hook.'
—What's a flounder?
—A big fish. Listen. 'Then the flounder said to him, "Please listen to me, Mr Fisherman, I beg you, let me go. I'm not a flounder at all but an enchanted prince. What good will it do you to kill me? I wouldn't taste good anyway. Put me back in the water and let me swim away."
'"Oh," said the man, "you needn't go on about it like that, a talking flounder I'd set free anyway."
'Then he put him back in the clear water and the flounder swam down to the bottom, leaving behind him a long streak of blood. Then the fisherman stood up and went back to his wife in the stinking hovel.'
Freddy stops reading.
—Go on, his son says.
—It's late, Freddy says. Now you must go to sleep.
—All right.
He kisses his son, puts out the light by his bed and feels his way to the door.
He knocks on his daughter's door. —Can I come in?
He kisses her: —Time to go to sleep, he says.
—Can I finish this chapter?
—How long is it?
—Not very long.

—All right. But promise you'll stop there.
—Promise.
—Good girl. Sleep well.
—You too.
—Becky? he says.
—Uhuh?
—Remember. You promised.
—Uhuh.
—All right, he says. Goodnight.

—May I ask you a question? says the man on the bench.
—Of course, Licia says.
—What, says the man, would you give to an eleven-year-old who has everything?
—Is it for a birthday? Licia asks.
—It is, the man says.
—And what are his interests?
—She is interested in everything, the man says.
—She has everything and she's interested in everything?
—That's right, the man says, turning on the bench and looking at her.
—Your daughter?
—Uhuh.
—And you don't know what she wants?
—I see her only rarely.
—Why's that?
—Her mother does not allow it.
—I'm afraid I can't help you, Licia says.
—I thought you might, the man says.
He looks down at his hands.
—Have you asked her? Licia asks.
—No, the man says. I wanted it to be a surprise.
—Of course.
—I thought, looking at you, that you might have something to suggest.
—I'm sorry.
—You can't help me?
—I think, she says, in those circumstances, one should always get what one wants oneself, or what one would have wanted oneself at that age, rather than trying to guess what the person one is giving the present to wants.
—You think so? the man says, looking at her.
—A book you would have liked at her age, Licia says. Or a kite. Something like that.
—What sort of a book would you have liked to have at eleven? the man asks.

—Leave me out of it, Licia says.
—Would you have liked to have a kite?
—Yes, Licia says. Very much.
—And you were never given one?
—No.
—I'm sorry.
—My brother didn't get one either.
—I was mad about bows and arrows at that age, the man says. Now it's all guns and aeroplanes and things.
—Is it?
—Or worse, the man says.
—Worse?
—Oh yes, the man says.
He looks down at his hands.
—And your daughter?
—I don't know.
She is silent.
—I don't see her very often, the man says. She has everything, he adds. Her mother sees to that.
—Lucky for her.
—Is it?
—Well isn't it?
The man is looking out over the Common.
—What did you give her last year? Licia asks him.
—Last year? I can't remember. I must have given her something, mustn't I?'
—And at Christmas?
—Christmas?
—Didn't you give her something at Christmas?
—Of course I did, the man says.
—And what was it?
—You know, the man says, turning to look at her, I can't remember. These things come and go, don't they. All the time. They're upon you all the time.
Licia stands up.
—You're going? the man says.
—Yes.
—I hope it's not because of me.
—No. I have to get back.
—I haven't been keeping you, have I?
—No. Not at all.
—I just thought, he says, looking at you, that you might have had an idea.

—Why looking at me?
　　—I don't know. It just struck me. That's why I asked you. I hope you're not offended.
　　—Offended? she says. Why?
　　—I don't know.
　　—I'm sure you'll think of something, she says.
　　—You are?
　　—I've got to go.
　　—I'm sorry to have kept you.
　　—You haven't, she says.
　　—It was a pleasure to talk to you.
　　—Goodbye.
　　The man stands up abruptly and extends his hand: —Goodbye.
　　She turns and walks away from him.

*

　　—It's not so much that, Julie says to her sister. It's his inconsiderateness I mind.
　　—I can't hear you, her sister says.
　　—I said it's the inconsiderateness I mind, Julie says.
　　—There's something wrong with the line, her sister says. I really can't hear you.
　　—I can hear you perfectly well, Julie says.
　　—What's that?
　　—I said there's nothing wrong with the line at my end.
　　—There's no need to shout, her sister says.
　　—When I don't shout you say you can't hear me.
　　—Well I can hear you now, her sister says. Go on.
　　—I can't go on, Julie says. Not if I have to shout.
　　—You don't have to shout, her sister says. Only talk clearly.
　　—I'm talking clearly, Julie says.
　　—That's fine, her sister says. Go on.
　　—I can't remember what I was saying.
　　—Inconsiderateness, her sister says.
　　—That's right, Julie says. One would have thought among civilised people a little consideration would have been the least to expect, I mean a minimal awareness of what needs –
　　—I'm sorry, her sister says. It's getting worse and worse.
　　—What is?
　　—What?
　　—What's getting worse and worse?
　　—What's that?
　　—Oh for God's sake! Julie says.

—Look, her sister says, I'll have to ring off anyway. I'll call you again later.
—I won't be there later.
—What's that?
—I said I won't be there later.
—I can't hear a word you're saying, her sister says. I'm going to put down the phone.
—Why were you shouting like that? her daughter asks her.
—There's something wrong with the line.
—Was that Aunt Emma?
—Yes. There's something wrong with the line. You shouldn't be listening to other people's conversation anyway.
—You were shouting.
—You should have blocked your ears.
—Blocked my ears?
—Put a finger in each ear, like that.
—And stuck out my tongue?
—If you wanted to.
—Like that?
—No. Like this.
—All right, Becky says. I'll try and remember.

*

—I have told you once and for all, Freddy says to his mother, I am not going to fetch him.
—I know dear.
—Then why go on about it?
—I'm sorry dear.
—He can take a taxi, Sam says. I'll pay.
—Dad'll pay, Freddy says.
—You know he wouldn't consider it.
—It's unbelievable, Sam says. The man is unbelievable.
The front door opens and they fall silent.
—I didn't know you were coming, Licia says when she sees her brother.
—I just dropped in.
She sits.
—You're tired? her father says.
—Uhuh.
—She's always tired, he says.
—Do you want a cup of tea? her mother asks.
—No thanks.
—Freddy?

—No thanks.
—I'm making a cup for myself.
—No thanks.
—Do you want some? she asks her husband.
—No thanks.
—I'm making some for myself.
—No thanks.
—Can I have a word with you? Freddy says to his sister. They step out into the garden.
—Well? she says.
—I saw Robin the other day.
—Oh yes?
—He sends his regards.
—Oh yes?
—He said he'd been trying to phone.
—That's right.
—Don't worry. I didn't encourage him.
—Thanks.
—I can't go on, Liss, he says. I can't go on with Petra.
—Why is that?
—I dread going there.
—Then why do you go?
—Maybe I won't.
—What do you want me to say?
—I don't know.
They sit on the bench.
—You want to talk about it? she says.
—There's this awful tension with Julie the whole time, he says. Then when I go round to Petra's it's just the same. Whatever I do she jumps on me. I'm not giving her enough time. I'm not giving her enough attention. It's driving me crazy.
—It doesn't sound a very good arrangement to me, Licia says.
—You don't like her.
—Why do you say that?
—You don't, do you?
—That's got nothing to do with it.
—It's driving me mad, he says.
She is silent.
—Both of them seemed so understanding at first, he says.
—That's the way it goes.
—I guess so.
—Shall we go in? I'm getting cold.
They move towards the house.

—You think I should end it? he asks.
—It's up to you.
—But if I were to ask your advice?
—But you're not.
—It wasn't like that at first, he says. She made me feel happy again and I didn't snap at Julie so much and everyone was better off.
—That's how it goes, Licia says.
—What's that supposed to mean?
They stand by the french windows.
—You're the only person I can talk to, he says.
—What do you want me to say?
—I just wanted to know what you thought.
—You know what I think.
—I just wanted to hear you say it.
—I can't say it, she says. You know that.
—Yes.
He looks at his watch. —I'd better go. I'm reading to Joe tonight.
—Still Grimm?
—Of course.
At the front door he says: —Thanks for listening.
—Oh . . .
—See you on Sunday.
—Uhuh.
—Are you going? his mother calls out.
—I've got to dash. I'm reading to Joe.
—You've hardly been here a minute.
—That's right. I've got to dash.
—I've hardly seen you.
—Ciao, he says to his sister. 'Bye, he calls out. I'll see you on Sunday.
—Won't you come in and say goodbye properly? his mother calls out.
He closes the front door, feels for the car keys in his trouser pocket.

*

—Did you go up to the Common? Ella asks her mother, handing her a cup of tea.
—There and back, Nina says.
—See anyone?
—Lots of dogs.
—What sort?

—Every sort, Nina says. Big ones and little ones.
—Did you see the Irish wolf-hound?
—Not today. But those two young boxers with the blonde girl were there.
—And the whippets?
—No, the whippets weren't there. Those two young boxers with their slim waists and then the Afghan hound.
—You never mentioned an Afghan hound.
—Yes, she says. With the tall man.
—Was he on a lead?
—No, Nina says. He was free. He was running about all over the place.
Ella takes her cup from her.
—I think I've always felt at home in England, Nina says, because of the dogs. Just like my childhood.
—And mine, Ella says.
—And yours, Nina says.
—Not Sam's, Ella says.
—No, Nina says, not Sam's.
Ella is silent.
—It's good for children to grow up with animals, Nina says. It gives them a sense of responsibility.
—Sam's frightened of them, Ella says. Because he didn't grow up with them.
—We always had them in our family, Nina says.
—He doesn't like cats either, Ella says.
—That's because he's allergic to them.
—Yes, Ella says. He's always been allergic to them.
—But he's not allergic to dogs.
—No. He just doesn't like them. He's frightened of them.
—You have to be brought up with them to like them, Nina says.
—Sam's family never had them, Ella says. He says Jews and dogs don't mix.
—That's not true, Nina says. Look at us.
—I told him that, Ella says.
—We never thought of ourselves as Jewish, Nina says. We always had English nannies in our family. Strict Anglicans. They brought us up to say our prayers. But when we grew up we all married Jews.
—I married a Jew, Ella says.
—But Freddy didn't.
—It's different for the children, Ella says. The only people we knew really were Jews.
—There were Greeks, Nina says.

—The only people of our sort, Ella says.
—There are plenty of Jews in England, Nina says.
—It's not the same thing.
—No, Nina says. It's more of a choice marrying a Jew in England.
Ella is silent.
—And we don't have that much in common with most of them anyway, Nina says.
—As long as they're happy, Ella says, what does it matter?
—What does happiness have to do with it? Nina says.
—You don't think it does?
—Happiness comes and goes, Nina says.
—Then what does matter?
—I don't know, Nina says. I know what doesn't but I'm not so sure about what does.

—I want to see the spiders, Becky says.
—I don't like the spiders, her father says.
—I do. I like the big furry one.
—The tarantula.
—Talantula, her brother says.
—Tarantula.
—That's what I said.
—No you didn't. You said talantula.
—They frighten me, Freddy says. They frighten Joe. You don't want to frighten Joe, do you?
—Yes I do.
—And me?
—You too.
—Becky, he says, you know what I think?
—What?
—I think you're a little bit frightened of them yourself.
—I'm not.
—But I think you rather like being frightened.
—Yes I do.
—I want an ice-cream, Joe says.
—I want to see the spiders.
—All right. Ice-cream first and then the spiders.
—Are you frightened of the spiders? she asks her brother.
—No, Joe says.
—He isn't frightened of them, she says. Only you are.
—I'm not ashamed to admit it.
—Why?
—Why what?
—Why are you frightened?
—I don't know. Does one know why one's frightened of something?
—You can stay here.
—No. I'll master my fear.
—I can take him. I know the way.
—Come on. Eat up. We'll have a quick look at the spiders and then have lunch.

—They're quite harmless, she says as they set off.
—No they're not, Freddy says. They're deadly poisonous.
—Then why does the man hold them in his hand?
—Because he's mad.
—Is he?
—He must be, to hold them in his hand.
—But he's the keeper.
—You must be mad to be a keeper of spiders.
—I want to be a keeper of spiders when I grow up.
—You're mad.
—I'm not.
—Yes you are.
—Here it is. Now don't be frightened. Hold my hand.

*

—Why wasn't the man there?
—Because it wasn't his day.
—Why was he there the last time?
—We were lucky. It was his day.
—What's his day?
—His day and his hour.
—What's his day Dad?
—Thursdays and Sundays.
—Why didn't we come on one of those days?
—Because we didn't know.
—Did we know the last time?
—No. We were lucky.
—Can I have an ice-cream? the little boy asks.
—No.
—Why not?
—Because you've had enough for one day.
—I'm hot.
—Ice-cream isn't good for you when you're hot.
—What day is it today?
—Wednesday.
—Can we come back on Thursday?
—No.
—Please Dad!
—No. You've had quite enough for one day.
—Can we come on Sunday?
—What are you grumbling about? You saw the spiders.
—I wanted to stroke the furry one.
—Another time.

—When?
—Soon.
—Oh Dad!
—I wanted to stroke it, she says. It's not the same seeing them behind the glass.
—Why don't you go and stroke that dog?
—It's not the same thing.
—It's much nicer.
– Can I finish your ice-cream? Joe asks his sister.
—No.
—All right, Freddy says. Go and buy another. But it's the last one you're having today.
—Why can't I come tomorrow and see the spiders if he's having another ice-cream?
—It's not the same thing.
—Why not Dad? Why not?
—You can have another ice too if you want.
—No.
—What do you want to see now?
—Nothing.
—You've seen all you want to see?
—Yes.
—Don't sulk.
—I'm not sulking.
—All right. We'll ask Joe what he wants to see.

*

—Why is it lying down like that?
—Because it's hot.
—Doesn't it like the heat?
—No. It's a polar bear. It likes the cold.
—Is that why it looks so unhappy?
—Yes.
—It doesn't like being shut up, his sister says.
—Where are the others?
—Inside.
—Can I have another ice-cream?
—No. I told you the last one was the last.
—Can I have a bun?
—We'll have one for tea.
—When are we having tea?
—When we've looked at a few more animals.
—I don't want to look at any more animals.

—What about you? he asks his daughter. Do you want to see any more animals?
—No.
—I told you not to sulk. It doesn't suit you.
—I'm not sulking.
—Yes you are.
—No I'm not.
—Come on, he says. We'll have tea and then go home.
—I don't want to go home.
—You don't want to look at any more animals and you don't want to go home. What do you want to do?
—I don't know.
—Do you want to have a go on the swings?
—Yes.
—All right.
—Can I have a bun first?
—No. We'll find some swings and then go and have tea and then home.
—Can we go and see the spiders again? Perhaps the man will be there.
—Why are you so obsessed with spiders? Don't you like the big animals?
—No.
—Why not? They're a lot nicer than spiders.
—They all look so sad.
—Not all of them.
—They don't like to be shut up.
—Do you think the spiders like it?
—They don't seem to mind, she says. Not like the lions and bears.
—I think you're right Becky, he says. I think you're absolutely right.

—Don't treat me like an invalid, Simon says. If there's one thing I hate it's being treated like an invalid.
—You are an invalid, Nina says.
—Hardly, Simon says. Hardly.
—But it hurts when you walk.
—Whenever I put some weight on it, Simon says. That's why I couldn't take the tube.
—How about the stairs?
—If you have to do something, Simon says, then you just grin and bear it, don't you?
—How was the traffic? Ella asks him.
—Negligible, Simon says. Negligible.
—I told Sam it wouldn't be a problem on a Sunday, Ella says.
—He knows all the byways, Simon says. That man knows London like the back of his hand.
—I told him there wouldn't be a problem, Ella says. He always imagines everything's going to be worse than it is.
—That's his nature, Simon says. What can you do? You can't change a man's nature you know.
—It's the same in the house, Ella says. The thought of doing anything like fixing a plug always throws him into a tizz but once he gets down to it he's highly efficient.
—He's a regular Englishman, Simon says. When it comes to DIY he's a regular Englishman.
—You went all the way there? Freddy says to his father. I can't believe it.
—It was simpler.
—Simpler than what?
—Arguing with your mother.
—And you're taking him all the way back?
—We'll see, Sam says.
—You're still walking up to the Common every day? Julie asks Nina.
—Up to the Common and back.
—That's the way, Julie says. There's nothing like regular exercise to keep one fit.

—I've taken some sort of walk every day of my life, Nina says. And I've never had a day's illness.

—That's the way, Julie says.

—Mind you, Nina says, only because I enjoy it. I wouldn't do it just for the sake of the exercise.

—It makes all the difference if you enjoy it, Julie says. It's like eating. I always say if you enjoy your food you benefit from it, if you don't, you don't. I always tell my clients, she says, only do what you enjoy, but do it in moderation.

—I bet they don't pay attention.

—Some of them do.

—But most of them don't.

—What can you do? Julie says. They're human beings, aren't they?

—We went to the zoo the other day, Becky says to her aunt.

—To see the spiders?

—The man who shows them wasn't there.

—That's a shame.

—It wasn't his day.

—I see.

—His day's Thursdays and Sundays. We didn't know that.

—But you saw them all the same.

—It's not the same as stroking them.

—Stroking them?

—He takes them out and holds them out to you, she says. The tarantulas. Then you can stroke them if you like.

Licia shudders. —I hate spiders, she says.

—Daddy hates them too.

—Everyone I know hates them, Licia says. Except you.

—I like them, Becky says. But I hate zoos.

—You hate zoos?

—Yes.

—Why?

—The animals look so sad in their cages.

—I know. I never go to the zoo myself any more.

—But you take us sometimes.

—I do it for you.

—Do you want to see the laburnum? Nina asks Julie. You get a very good view of it from my window.

—Later perhaps, Julie says.

—Much better than from the garden.

—I'd put him in a taxi, Freddy says. You can pay for it this end.

—You know what he's like with taxis.

—If you put him inside and shut the door he isn't going to get out.
—He's capable of it.
—Let's see him do it.
—You know what your mother would say.
—Let her say it.
—You don't have to live with it.
—True.
—You can touch so long as you don't press, Simon says to Joe.
—Like that?
—Ouch.
—You said touch it.
—Gently. Gently.
—Does it hurt then?
—Yes. It's pretty swollen, isn't it?
—Not very.
—Not very? What do you want? A balloon?
—I thought it would be much more swollen than that. When Daddy told me.
—It was. It's starting to subside.
—What's subside?
—Go down. You see that mark there? It was all swollen right up to there.
—Right up to there?
—That's right.
—Is Robin still pestering you? Freddy asks his sister.
—Yes.
—I did my best.
—I know.
—I can put it a bit more strongly next time I see him.
—No no. Let him ring. Ella likes to talk to him.
—Does she?
—She says he's a gentleman.
—What does she know about it?
—She trusts her instinct.
—It's extraordinary, isn't it, he says. After all these years of her instinct letting her down and she still trusts it.
—The triumph of hope over experience.
—More like the triumph of cliché over intelligence.
She sits down next to Simon. —They've left you all on your own?
—What do you expect my dear? An old man and with a sprained ankle to boot.
—To boot?

—How are you?
—Fine.
—I feel terrible.
—You don't look so bad.
—I feel terrible inside.
—Don't we all?
—But with me it corresponds to reality, he says. You should see what I feel like inside.
—You mean it doesn't with me?
—Did I say that Liss? How do I know what you feel like inside? I hear things, of course.
—From Ella?
—Who else?
—What does she say?
—That you're unhappy. That you've lost your sense of direction. That sort of thing.
—You believe her?
—Why not? Aren't we all unhappy? Haven't we all lost our sense of direction? Why should you be the exception?
—It does me good talking to you, she says.
—That's why I came.
—Just for me?
—Just for you.
—Do you think it's true?
—What?
—What you've just said.
—Of course. But then the opposite's true as well. Maybe deep down we all know where we're going. Maybe deep down we're all quite happy with our lot. Who can tell?
—That's cheering, she says.
—Your grandfather used to say: Not Know Thyself but Shema Yisroel.
—Meaning what?
—Meaning looking inwards is a waste of time but you must do what God put you on earth to do.
—And you believe that?
—Of course. Every other day.
—He believed it?
—What does it mean believed? He said it. He got it I think from Martin Buber.
—So he didn't believe it? He said it like a talisman?
—The trouble with your grandfather was he had no sense of humour. In that he was very like Martin Buber I understand.

—Maybe it's not such a good thing to have a sense of humour.

—Maybe not. But not having it can be hard on other people. And if you're a great moralist as well it puts a big strain on personal relations. Why? Because everybody around you recognises the truth of what you're saying but since none of them can live up to it they start to hate themselves and then they hate you for making them hate themselves and everything gets very difficult.

—That happened with you?

—The trouble with Buber, Simon says, is that he was more of a German Protestant than he realised. Kafka sensed that in him, you know. That do-goody morality coupled with a lack of a sense of humour and a constant awareness of himself as an important person.

—And grandfather was like that?

—Exactly.

—That must have been tough on you.

—It was tough on all his brothers and sisters. But he was a great man. You couldn't help admiring him.

—Every other day? she asks.

—Every other day.

—That's the right kind of balance, isn't it?

—The trouble with setting up idols, Simon says, is that when you start to doubt them you have nothing left.

—And you? You have something left?

—No.

—As bleak as that?

—Every other day.

—Sam's going to take you home now Simon, Ella says, sitting down with them.

—Ella, your cooking gets better and better.

—You always say that.

—I'm struck by it every time I eat here.

Licia gets up.

—Did you talk to Mother? Ella asks him.

—I didn't get the chance.

—She'll be hurt.

—Nah, Simon says. She hasn't even noticed.

—Of course she has.

—What can I do with this ankle of mine? he says. If she wanted to talk to me all she had to do was come over and do so.

—You were hobbling about all right a few minutes ago.

—Me?

—Don't think I didn't see you.

—Anyway, we don't have much to say to each other any more.

—Of course you do.

—Anyway, he says, I talked to everyone else. I had a good time. As always.

—I'm glad.

—I wouldn't do without these lunches of yours for anything.

—Now go and get ready. Sam wants to take you home.

—I wouldn't keep him waiting. He's a busy man. I was saying to Ella that I wouldn't keep you waiting, he says to Sam, who has come to stand over them. You're a busy man.

—I want to get you back before the rush hour starts, Sam says.

—Rush hour? On Sundays?

—You don't drive, Sam says. You don't know what it's like.

—You're a pessimist, Simon says. How much traffic did we meet when we came?

—That's because I kept off the main roads.

—Then that's what you'll do now.

—Even the side-roads will be busy now, Sam says.

—He's a pessimist, Simon says to his niece. He doesn't know what a genius he is at avoiding the traffic.

—Are you ready? Sam says.

—I'll just hobble off and have a wash.

—Do you want a hand getting out of the chair?

—No. I can manage. With my stick I can manage. If you'll bear with me.

He gets up slowly.

—In a second I'll be with you, he says.

—Good morning, the man says.
—Good morning.
—May I?
He sits down on the bench beside her.
—How are you?
—I'm well. And you?
—We talked the other day, he says.
—I know, she says.
They look out over the Common.
—Did you find something? she asks.
—Find something?
—For your little girl.
—Ah, he says. Yes.
—And won't you tell me what?
—I seem to remember you suggested a kite.
—You bought her a kite?
—I liked the idea.
He is silent.
She asks: —Do you have any other children?
—I'm not married, he says.
—No no. I mean . . .
—Are you? he asks.
—No.
—Why?
—Why aren't I married?
—Yes.
—I don't know, she says. I haven't met anyone I wanted to marry.
—But if you met him you'd marry him.
—I don't know, she says.
—There you are, he says.
—What do you mean, there I am?
He is lost in thought.
—What do you mean, she says again, there I am?
Then she too retreats into her thoughts.

Finally she says: —I get very tired these days. I don't know what's the matter with me but I get very tired.

He turns and looks at her along the bench.

—I don't do anything but I feel tired all the time.

—I'm not a doctor, he says.

—I didn't mean—

He is lost to her again.

—I had to give up my job, she says.

—You did?

—I was too tired to continue. I was too tired to see the point of it.

—It's the air, he says.

—The air? You mean here in London?

—Everywhere, he says. It's the same everywhere. It's the pollutants.

—They make one tired?

—They affect the immune system, he says.

—I didn't know that.

—Oh yes they do, he says.

—I wasn't disputing it. I just said I didn't know.

—Have you looked at people? he says.

—What do you mean looked at them?

—It's the PVCs he says.

—The—?

—They pollute everything.

—I don't think—

—Have you looked into their eyes?

—My brother's got terrific energy, she says. He—

—Just walk down the street, he says. Look into people's eyes. Then you'll see.

—I know what you mean, she says.

—You've done that?

—I know what you mean.

He is silent, looking out over the Common.

—I try to read a book, she says. But I can't seem to go on. I used to read a lot.

—I know the feeling, he says.

—Even when it's by an author I used to like.

He looks out over the Common.

—Even when it's by someone whose books I used to devour, she says.

—You see that tree there? he says.

—Which one?

—There on the left.

—With the short trunk?
—It was struck by the hurricane, he says. Every single branch came off. But it held on. It fought back.
—Is that an allegory? she says.
—Allegory?
—Should I take it as an example?
—An example?
—I thought you were holding it up as an example.
—I was pointing out a fact.
—You were here during the hurricane?
—On the Common?
—No. Living here.
—I don't live here, he says.
—Oh?
—No, he says. I don't live here.
—Where do you live then?
—Not here.
—But this is where you come.
—I like it here.
—There are nicer open spaces in London.
—I don't *only* come here, he says.
—No. Of course not.
—This is *one* of the places I come to, he says.
She is silent.
—Just *one* of them, he says.
She looks at her watch. —I have to go, she says.
—Already?
—I have to.
She stands up. —Goodbye.
He stands with her. —I'm not driving you away?
—No of course not. Goodbye.
He holds out his hand: —Goodbye.
She shakes his hand and turns. He sits down again in his place, looking out over the Common.

*

—It's the humiliation, Julie says.
—There are worse things than humiliation, her sister says.
—Of course there are, Julie says.
—Would you like another coffee? her sister asks.
—Please.
She stares out of the window at the people passing by in the street. Her sister returns with the coffee.

—He doesn't talk to me any more, she says.
—Did he ever have anything interesting to say?
—That's not the point. People don't talk to each other to say interesting things.
—Sure, her sister says.
—You know what I mean?
—Sure, her sister says. Sure.
—Don't say sure like that, Julie says.
—I'm sorry.
—I don't know when it began, Julie says.
—One never does, her sister says.
—One day we were getting along fine and then this.
—He's got someone else?
—Of course he's got someone else, Julie says. But it isn't serious.
—Well then.
—Well then what?
—If it isn't serious.
—It's serious between us, Julie says.
—It'll blow over.
—It won't, Julie says. It just gets worse and worse.
—That's what you always say.
—Not like this, Julie says.
—Things happen, her sister says. You hit a patch of bad weather and then it's behind you.
—And you're the stronger for it.
—I didn't say that, her sister says.
She toys with her coffee.
—What about that book he was writing? her sister asks.
—He's not writing it.
—There you are then.
—What do you mean?
—He's having problems with his book and he takes it out on you.
—He's not having problems with it. He's just not writing it.
—That's what I'm saying. He needs to blame somebody so he blames you.
—It's not me I'm concerned with, Julie says. It's the children.
—Don't give me that, her sister says. It's you you're concerned with and quite right too.
—It's the children, Julie says.
—The one thing you can't say about Freddy is that he's a bad father, her sister says.
—I didn't say that, Julie says. I said the atmosphere wasn't good for them.

—They won't notice.
—Of course they notice.
—Believe me, all this about children being sensitive to any tension between their parents is a lot of —.
—You think so? It's a fact that seventy-eight per cent of disturbed children come from broken homes.
—Look, her sister says, I'm sorry. I have to go.
—You don't want another coffee?
—I've got to go. I'm sorry.
She stands up. —Give it time, she says. It'll sort itself out.
—No it won't, Julie says. Not this time.
—Not if you take that attitude, her sister says.
She kisses her. —Be strong, she says.

*

—She's tired, Ella says.
—At her age? Sam says.
—What has age to do with it?
—At her age you don't have a right to be tired, he says. You hear that? he says to his daughter.
—Yes, Licia says.
—Leave her alone, Ella says.
—Why should she be tired? Sam says. Can you explain to me why she should be tired?
—She just is, Ella says.
—All she's done is sit on a bench on the Common for an hour. How does one get tired sitting on a bench?
—Perhaps you should go and see a doctor, Ella says to her daughter.
—She's been to the doctor, Sam says. He didn't find anything wrong with her.
—Maybe another doctor would find something.
—And if he doesn't? We try another and another till one of them finds?
—Maybe she should try one more.
—You know what doctors are for, Sam says. They're for people who are ill. Not people who are tired.
—Maybe she's ill.
—You think you're ill? he asks his daughter.
—I'm tired, she says.
—There you are, he says to his wife. She's not ill, she's tired.
—Maybe being tired is an illness.
—What does it mean, an illness?

—Maybe there's something she could take for it.
—I'll tell you what she could take, he says. She could take a job.
—Leave her alone, Ella says.
—I'm saying it for her sake.
—I know you are.
—It beats me, he says, why anyone should throw in a good job they've trained all their life for just to sit around at home and complain.
—She's not complaining.
—What's she doing then?
—You asked her what was the matter with her and she gave you a reply, Ella says.
—What sort of a reply is that? he says. It's meaningless. Strictly meaningless.
—Leave her alone.
—I'm not forcing her to do anything, Sam says. Nothing she doesn't want. I'm only saying it for her sake. If she gets a job she'll stop feeling tired. She won't be thinking about herself and how tired she is the whole time. She'll have a goal in life. That's all I'm saying.

*

—I'm sorry, Freddy says.
—And how am I supposed to feel?
He is silent.
—I asked you how I was supposed to feel, Petra says.
He is silent.
—Are you still there? she says.
—Yes, he says.
—I thought perhaps you'd gone away.
—No, he says.
—You don't have anything else to say to me?
He is silent.
—You know what this means? she says.
He is silent.
—Are you still there? she says.
—Yes, he says.
—I take it your silence implies you know what it means, she says.
—I'm sorry, he says.
—You know, she says, the trouble with you is that you behave like a bastard but want to be seen as caring and compassionate.
He is silent.
—Like all men, she says.
—I'm sorry Petra, he says.

—At least if you'd told me to my face I could have hit you, she says. She starts to laugh.

He waits.

—Are you still there? she says when she has stopped laughing.

—Yes.

—What about tomorrow?

—I'm sorry.

—Sorry what?

—I can't.

—And the day after?

—I'm sorry.

—I just wanted to get it quite clear, she says.

He waits.

—Aren't you going to say something? she asks.

—What is there to say?

—What is there to say? Is that all you can say?

He waits.

—You make me laugh, she says. You really make me laugh.

She starts to cry.

—I'm sorry, he says.

He waits, listening to her crying, then he puts down the phone.

*

—Then, Nina says, Nanny would dress us up and we would go out to tea with the Australian officers. We were great friends with the Australian officers. And the New Zealand officers.

—Were there a lot of them? Licia asks.

—The place was swarming with them, Nina says. They were all there waiting to go and fight in Europe.

—Why did they invite you to tea?

—I think we reminded them of their own children, Nina says.

—Did you ever hear from any of them again?

—No, Nina says. When we asked Nanny what had become of them she said they had all died at Gallipoli.

—All of them?

—That's what she said. All of them.

—What did they give you for tea?

—English cakes, Nina says. Delicious English cakes. I mean, she says, they were delicious because they were part of that special treat, having tea with our officer friends in their nice new uniforms. I probably wouldn't touch those cakes now, all pink icing and jam.

—They weren't like the cakes you had at home?

—We never had cakes at home, Nina says. Only *petits fours*.

—How did you dress when you went to tea with the Australian officers?

—We had bows in our hair. Big bows. And shoes with buckles.

—And you tied the bows yourselves?

—Good heavens no! Nina says. We couldn't even brush our own hair till we were twelve.

She stares out of the window. —We were completely hopeless, she says. It took Nanny's death to catapult us into real life.

—Your life seems much more real than mine, Licia says.

—That's always the case, Nina says. Other people's lives always seem far more real than one's own. What you have to remember is that for other people your life is far more real than theirs.

—Not mine, Licia says.

—Yours too.

—I can't believe it.

—You've got to, Nina says. Otherwise you can't go on.

—Sometimes I feel I can't go on, Licia says.

—All young people feel that, Nina says. That's the advantage of getting old. You find you can.

—I'm not a young person, Licia says.

—Some people feel it sooner than others, Nina says. But everyone feels it at some point in their lives.

—You too? Licia asks.

—Of course, Nina says. Do you think I'm any different from anyone else?

—Yes, Licia says. Of course I do.

—Her best friend, Freddy says.
—Who?
—Nancy Fisher.
—How did it happen?
—It's unbelievable really, Freddy says. She was standing on the back of the bus, waiting to get off. In Islington. And another bus hit it full on.
—Oh my God, Licia says.
—Everyone on the platform was killed, Freddy says.
– Oh my God, Licia says.
—They're investigating what happened, Freddy says. You can imagine how she feels.
—I can't believe it, Licia says.
—Nancy's brother rang with the news, Freddy says. The funeral's on Friday.
—Was it the brakes? Licia asks.
—She's just shut herself up in her room, Freddy says. She isn't even crying.
—And the children?
—I've told them she died. I didn't go into details.
—She had children? Licia asks.
—No, thank God.
—Nobody else was hurt?
—I told you. They were all killed on the platform.
—I mean pedestrians.
—I don't know. An inquiry is under way.
—You want me to come round? Take the children out?
—No no. It's just Julie who's affected really. I have to say I wasn't overfond of her myself. She's sitting in the bedroom not saying anything.
—I'm sorry, Licia says.
—These things happen.
—Yes but still.
—Right there in Middle Street, Freddy says. It's unbelievable.
—How close were they?

—You mean the buses?
—No no. She and Julie.
—She was her best friend.
—It's unbelievable.

*

Freddy opens the bedroom door. —Can I get you anything? he asks.
 Julie is sitting on the edge of the bed, staring down at the carpet.
 —A cup of coffee? Freddy says. A cup of tea?
 —No, she says.
 —Is there anyone you want me to ring up?
 —No, she says.
 —You're OK?
 —Yes.
He closes the door.
 —Is Mummy all right? Becky asks.
 —Yes. She just needs to be by herself a bit.
 —Can we go to the park?
 —Now?
 —Yes.
 —How about Joe?
 —He wants to go too.
 —Do you want to go to the park?
 —No.
 —What do you want to do?
 —I want to stay here.
 —What do you want to do here?
 —I want to see Mummy.
 —You can't see her at the moment. She needs to be by herself.
 —Why?
 —She's had a shock.
 —Because Nancy's dead?
 —Yes.
 —Come on, Becky says. Let's go to the park.
 —I don't want to. I want to stay here.
 – Spoilsport.
 —Come on, Freddy says. Let's go down to the swings.
 He knocks on the bedroom door and opens it again: —I'm taking them down to the park.
 Julie sits on the edge of the bed looking down at the carpet.
 —OK?
She doesn't answer.
 —Will you be all right? he asks.

—Yes.
—OK. We won't be long.
He closes the door again. —Come on, he says.
—I want to stay here, Joe says.
—You can't. Mummy wants to be by herself.
—I want to stay here.
—Come on. Put on your jacket. It's getting chilly.
Outside the sun is covered by a veil of clouds. —Give me your hands, he says to the children.
—Was the bus coming up behind the other one? Becky asks as they wait for the green man.
—Yes.
—Didn't it see it?
—Nobody knows. They're trying to find out.
—Perhaps the driver was drunk.
—Perhaps.
—Can we go on the big swings?
—If you're careful.
—Will you swing me?
—We'll see.
—It's lucky Nancy didn't have any children, Becky says.
—Yes. Very lucky.
—It would be terrible for them if she did.
—Luckily she didn't.
—But it's terrible for her mother.
—Yes.
—And her father.
—Yes.
—What about the other people who died?
—What about them?
—Did they have any children?
—I don't know.
—It will be terrible for them if they did.
—Come on. Let's go to the swings.
—Let go my hand.
—I'm sorry. I didn't realise I was still holding it. Come on Joe, he says. We can go down the slide.
—I don't want to go down the slide.
—Will you have a swing then?
—No.
—Are you going to sulk then?
—I'm not sulking.
—All right. I'm sorry.

—Can we go back and see Mummy?
—Not yet. She wants to be by herself a bit.
—Will you swing me Daddy?
—All right. Hold on.
—Come on, Daddy!
—Come on, he says to his son. We'll go and swing Becky.
—Can you swing me too?
—Of course. First Becky and then you. Now stand back.
—Higher, Becky says.
—Hold on tight.
—I'm holding on.
—OK. Here we go.

—Would you say you were a summer person yourself? the man asks.
—What do you mean a summer person?
—I mean do you feel yourself growing or shrinking during the summer?
—I've never thought of it like that, Licia says.
—Which? the man says.
—I don't know.
—Perhaps you're an autumn person, the man says. Solitary people often are.
—I'm not solitary, Licia says.
—I have to say that personally I like the summer, the man says. Especially the sorts of summers we've been having recently. Yet I also know that in the summer I shrink.
—Physically? Licia asks.
—Physically of course, the man says. One eats less when it's hot. One wears fewer clothes. One is altogether less bulky than one is in the winter. But I mean spiritually too. Psychologically. In the winter my mental horizons expand. In the summer they contract.
—That's very interesting, Licia says.
—It's a fact, the man says.
—Does it worry you? Licia asks him.
—No, he says. It would only worry me if I thought the summers would never end.
—And you would stay shrunk for ever.
—Shrunk?
—Well . . .
—I know what you mean, he says.
—That's not likely to happen, is it? Licia says. Even with all this global warming.
—I don't know what I'd do, the man says. If I thought there was a chance of that.
—You feel you lose touch with yourself in the summer?
—Exactly. I enjoy it but I lose touch with myself. I do not know who I am any more. I call that a shrinking of the self.
She is silent.

—Even with an effort, he says, I find it difficult to recall who I am. What I want. Why I want it. And all because of the heat.
—My mother grew up in a much hotter climate, Licia says.
—Italy?
—No.
—Greece?
—No.
—That is why the Mediterranean peoples are so uncomplicated, the man says. Why the English and the Germans are so very introverted and complicated.
—You think it can all be put down to the climate?
—Largely, he says. Don't you?
—I don't know. I've never thought of it.
—The Italians are like lizards, he says. They bask in the sun and when it gets hot, scuttle into the shade. The Germans are like moles. They dig down and hide. And when they try to act like lizards they make fools of themselves.
—You do generalise, she says.
—There is a place for generalisations, he says.
—And the English?
He turns on the bench and looks at her.
—And the English? she says again, facing him.
—Do you come here in the winter? he asks her.
—Yes of course. Why?
—I wondered.
—And you?
—Not so much, he says.
—Why is that?
—It depends on whether I have time on my hands or not.
—And usually you don't.
—Don't what?
—Have time on your hands.
—It all depends, he says.
—But at the moment you do.
—At present, yes, he says.
—So do I.
—We both have time on our hands, he says.
—Yes.
—Yes, he says.

*

—My wife's best friend was killed the other day, Freddy says.
—Killed? How?

—She was standing on the platform of a bus, waiting to get off, when another bus came up from behind and rammed right into it.

—Good heavens! she says.

—Everyone on the platform was killed, Freddy says.

—How dreadful! she says. How dreadful for your wife.

—It was no doubt worse for her friend.

—Yes of course, she says. But it must have been a terrible shock for your wife.

—It was a terrible shock, Freddy says.

—How is she coping?

—She's in a state of shock, he says.

—I should think so, she says.

—She is either completely silent or she breaks out into fits of hysteria, he says.

—How dreadful! she says.

—It's hard for the children, he says.

—Of course it is.

—It's the shock, he says. The unexpectedness of it.

—Of course it is, she says.

—What would you like for dessert? he says.

—I need to see the menu.

—Of course, he says.

—If I can be of any help . . . she says, as he motions to the waiter.

—How kind of you.

—No, she says. I mean it. I'm quite good in crises.

—I'm sure you are, he says.

—I think I'll have the fruit salad.

—Nothing more exotic?

—I'll stick to the fruit salad.

—Perhaps, he says, if you have the time, you could help me take out the children one of these afternoons.

—I'd love to.

—Good.

—If your wife wouldn't mind.

—How could she mind? You'd be doing both of us a favour.

—Then I'd love to.

—And . . . coffee? he asks as the waiter returns.

He orders.

—If you get out your diary, he says to her, then we can see what we can arrange.

*

—I'm worried about Simon, Ella says.
—Why? Sam says.
—This fall seems to have done something to him.
—I didn't notice, Sam says.
—He seems to have lost some of his zest.
—Zest? Sam says. Simon?
—You know what I mean, she says.
—No, he says.
—He was always getting about and going to lectures and things, she says. Now he lies in bed all day and doesn't even read.
—Maybe he's thinking.
—He was always telling me what books I ought to read, she says. He was always a great educator. Now he just complains about his aches and pains.
—Maybe he'll stop trying to tell other people how to live their lives, Sam says.
—He was always so full of ideas, Ella says. So full of suggestions.
—Maybe it's just a question of *reculer pour mieux sauter*, Sam says.
—I hope you're right.
—I don't, he says.
—It was always the British Museum for a lecture on Mexican sculpture or Chatham House for a Round Table on Muslim Fundamentalism. Now he just goes on about the pains in his chest.
—I thought it was his ankle.
—No, she says. His chest.
—But it was his ankle he sprained, not his chest.
—Oh yes, she says. But recently he's been complaining of pains in the chest.
—He was always like that, he says.
—Like what?
—Complaining of this and that.
—That's his way, she says.
—That's what I'm saying.
—But it was never like this, she says.
—I wouldn't worry, he says. He'll outlive us all.
—I just don't like to see the change that's come over him, she says.
—You just don't like to see change in any shape or form, he says.
—That's true, she says.
—Who does? he says.
—That's true, she says.

—'Then,' Freddy reads, 'the fisherman stood up and went back to his wife in the stinking hovel.'

'"Well, husband," said the wife, "didn't you catch anything today?"

'"No," said the man. "I did catch a flounder, but he said he was an enchanted prince so I let it go."'

—What's a flounder?

—I told you. A big fish.

—Like a whale?

—No. Much smaller.

—How big then?

—About like that, I think. Now can I go on?

—Yes.

—'"You mean you didn't wish for anything?" said the wife.

'"No," said the man. "What do I want to wish for?"

'"Ach," said the wife, "it's terrible to have to live in a stinking hovel all one's life, it's damp and it smells and the rain comes in through the roof. You could have wished for a little cottage for us, at least. Go on back and call to it. Tell it we want to have a little cottage. It'll surely grant you that."

'"Ah," said the man, "what should I go back for then? It's not that kind of prince."

'"You caught it," said the wife, "and you let it swim off again; it'll surely do what you ask. Go on right back and ask it."

'The man didn't want to go at all, but he didn't want to oppose his wife, so he went on down to the sea.

'When he got there the sea was all green and yellow and not nearly so clear. So he went and stood by it and said:

> "Munntje munntje timper tee
> Flounder, flounder in the sea –
> My good wife, dame Ilsebill,
> Wills not what I'd have her will."

'Then the flounder came swimming up and said: "Well, what does she want then?"

'"Ah," said the man, "you remember I caught you, and my wife says I ought to wish for something. She doesn't want to live in a stinking hovel any longer, she wants a little cottage."

'"Just go on home," the flounder said. "She's got her cottage already."'

Freddy stops reading and looks down at his son. His eyes are closed and his breathing is deep and steady. He draws the blanket over his shoulders, puts out the light and tiptoes out of the room.

He enters his daughter's room. She is curled up with her book under the blankets.

He sits on the bed. She gives no sign of having noticed him.

—You'll put out the light soon? he says.
—I just want to finish this.
—Why don't you hold the book up over the blankets?
—I like it like this.
—How can you see anything?

She ignores him.

—Don't read too late, he says.
—No.

He bends over and kisses her head through the blankets:
—Goodnight darling.
—Goodnight.

*

Julie is sitting in the kitchen staring into space.
—How are you feeling? he asks her.
—All right.

He sits down.
—No better?
—All right.
—Can I get you anything?
—No.
—Sure?
—Sure.
—Would you like me to get supper?
—As you like.

He gets up and goes to the fridge. —Did you talk to your mother? he asks.
—Yes, she says.

He starts to peel the vegetables. —It'll be better now, he says. Now the funeral's over.
—Yes, she says.
—You need to pull yourself together, he says.

—Yes, she says.
—Can I get you a drink?
—No.
—Mind if I have one myself?
She is silent.
—You're sure I can't get you one?
She looks up at him. —Just leave me alone, she says.
—Sorry, he says. Just trying to help.

*

—It won't shut properly, Nina says.
—Yes it will.
—I felt a draught in my back all night.
—It's shut, Sam says. You must have imagined it.
—I tell you I felt a draught. You'll have to get someone to mend it.
—There's nothing wrong with it, Sam says. He throws the window open then closes it firmly to demonstrate.
—I tell you I felt a draught, Nina says. Do you think I made it up?
—No of course not.
—Then be so kind as to get someone to see to it.
—Have a look for yourself, he says. It's shut as tight as it can be.
—Do you think I'm making it up?
—Sometimes one imagines things.
—I tell you I felt it.
—Well look for yourself. It's shut tight.
—I asked Liss to shut it for me, Nina says. Because there was such a wind blowing. But the wind still got through. I could feel it on my back all night.
—Put your hand here, Sam says, guiding her. Can you feel anything?
—Do you think I made it up?
—I'm just saying there's no point in getting someone to look at it.
—Do you want me to get a stiff neck?
—Of course not.
—Well then.
—Just put your hand there. Feel.
—The wind's died down.
—What do you want me to do?
—Get a man to see to it.
—Were you covered up properly?
—Of course I was, she says. But the room's so small. If a draught

comes in through the window you feel it no matter how well covered you are.

—You always said it was such a big room Nina.

—No, she says. It's so small I feel as if I'm right up against the window.

—But you always said it was such a big room.

—I can't have said that.

—But you did. You always have.

—Then I didn't know what I was talking about.

—Anyway, the wind's died down now.

—But what if it starts up again?

—Look. It's shut tight.

—I don't want to look. I tell you I felt it right there on my neck.

—All right, he says. I'll see what I can do.

—Get the young man who came last time, she says. He'll know what to do.

—I'll see, he says.

—If the wind gets up again I'll freeze to death, she says.

—I thought you always kept the window open at night anyway, he says.

—Not when the wind's blowing. I'd like to but I can't. Not with a room as small as this. I'd freeze to death.

—I'll see what I can do, he says.

—What did *you* do this morning? the man asks.
—Me? Licia says. Nothing.
—I was riding on the Epsom Downs at six, the man says.
—You were?
—There's nothing better than a ride in the mist on a spring morning, the man says.
—I didn't know you rode, she says.
—Nothing better, he says. Nothing more satisfying.
—You have your own horse?
—The smoke from the horse's nostrils mingles with the mist rising off the Downs, he says. And the thunder of his hooves is the only sound to be heard.
—You have your own horse?
—Does it surprise you?
—Yes, she says.
—Why is that?
—I don't know. I somehow didn't imagine.
—Perhaps you would come out with me one morning.
—Oh I don't ride, she says quickly.
—One can learn, he says.
—I don't think so.
—Oh yes. Anyone can. Horses are docile creatures.
—I mean it's not the kind of thing I think of myself doing.
—Perhaps that's only because you haven't done it.
—Perhaps, she says. But it doesn't really tempt me.
—Some people are frightened of horses, he says. Of their size. Of their strength. But horses are docile creatures.
—It doesn't tempt me.
—Pity.
—You go often? she asks him.
—Whenever I get the chance.
—And how often is that?
—It depends.
—On what?
—On many factors.

—I prefer to walk, she says.

He gazes down at his hands. —There isn't another sensation like it, he says.

She is silent.

—You have to have experienced it to understand.

—Perhaps, she says.

—You don't sound convinced.

—I only said perhaps, she said.

—Of course, he says, it's different if you've done it all your life.

—I suppose so, she says.

—Before breakfast, he says. The best time is before breakfast. When the day is still young and the Downs themselves still seem to be in the process of waking up.

She is silent.

—Nothing like it, he says.

—I believe you, she says.

—You have to have experienced it to know what I mean.

—One could say that about everything.

—True, he says.

—And your daughter? she says. You take her out with you?

—Start 'em young, he says. That's the secret. Then it becomes second nature to them.

—Walking is second nature to me, she says.

—Brush aside any thought of fear, he says. Make it seem the most natural thing in the world. And so for them it is.

—I don't know where I got it from, she says. Neither of my parents cares very much for walking.

—If they fall, he says, pick 'em up, stick 'em on the horse again. Don't give 'em time to think about it.

—Isn't it dangerous? she asks.

—Only if you're afraid, he says. Only if you give yourself time to be afraid.

—That's what I would do, she says. I would always be waiting to fall.

—You can't tell, he says. You can't tell till you've tried. You might find you were a natural.

—Not me, she says.

—Why not you?

—It's not in my temperament.

—You can't tell, he says. Not till you've had a go.

*

—How are they treating you? Ella asks her uncle Simon.

—How do you think?

—You like the nurses?
—I hate everything about the place.
—Aren't they looking after you properly?
—What did I pay my contribution all my working life for if it's not to be looked after properly when I fall ill? Simon says.
—It looks very clean, Ella says. It looks very cheerful.
—You'd say that about a crematorium, Ella, he says.
—I wouldn't.
—Can't you smell? he says. The place stinks.
—It doesn't.
—It stinks of sickness and despair, he says.
—No it doesn't, she says.
—I want to get out of here, he says. Ella, you've got to help me.
—They'll discharge you when you're all right, she says. You've just got to be patient.
—I'm all right now, he says. I'll write to my MP. Get me some writing paper.
—What for?
—Ella, he says. For the love of God. Get me out of here. I don't care how you do it, but do it.
—Quiet, she says. Don't get excited.
—Am I screaming?
—You're on the mend, she says. That's what the doctor says. It's just a question of patience.
—I'm not a patient type of person, he says. You know me, Ella.
—I know, she says. Just make an effort. It doesn't help to fret, you know.
—I want to get out of here, he says. I'm frightened of never getting out.
—Have you got enough to read? she asks him.
—I can't read.
—Why not? You were always a great reader.
—I can only read in an environment I'm familiar with. I can't read with all this going on around me.
—Everything seems very quiet to me, she says.
—You should hear it at night.
—Don't they keep people quiet?
—They shout at me when I ask them to be quiet.
—I'm sure they don't.
—You don't know anything about it, Ella, he says. You don't have to spend your nights in here.
—Quiet, she says. Quiet.

—Ella, he says. I'm begging you. Go and talk to the doctor. Tell him it's bad for me to stay here. Tell him I need to get home.

—They'll send you home when you're ready to go home, she says.

—You're taking their side?

—Of course I am, she says. They want you cured and out of here as much as you do.

—I'll tell you what they want, he says. They want me out of here all right, but feet first so they never have to spend another penny on me again.

—Don't talk like that, she says. You upset me.

—And me? he says. You think I'm not upset?

—Of course you're upset, she says. No one likes to be in hospital. But thank goodness you're in good hands.

—I'm in terrible hands, he says.

—You're just making yourself ill.

—Of course I am, he says. The longer I stay here the iller I get.

—Please, Simon, she says.

—What's happening to me? he says. What's to become of me?

—You had a mild stroke, she says. Now you're recovering. Soon you'll be as fit as a fiddle and back home leading your own life.

—You're so literal Ella, he says.

—Am I? she says.

—It's a terrible shock, a thing like this, Simon says. I'll never get over it.

—Of course you will, she says. Once they let you go you'll have forgotten it in no time.

—Not as long as I live, he says. And that won't be very long if they have their way.

—Don't talk like that, she says.

—Ella, he says. I'm asking you for the last time. For the sake of your father's memory. Take me home.

—I can't, Simon, she says.

—Why not?

—We have to wait till you're discharged.

—They'll never discharge me.

—When you're ready to be discharged they'll discharge you, she says. You think they don't know their job?

—I'm damn well sure they don't.

—Of course they do, she says. What do you think they have all that training for?

—All the training in the world can't put them in my shoes, he says.

—The more you fret the longer it'll take, she says.

—So I'm supposed to lie here and *submit*? he says.

—Be reasonable, Simon.

—Reason and I have parted company for good, he says.

—You've got to control yourself, she says. I'm going to leave you now but I want you to promise to try and control yourself.

He closes his eyes.

—Simon, she says.

He does not answer.

—I'll come and see you tomorrow, she says.

She pats his head. —Goodbye dear, she says.

He does not answer. His eyes remain firmly closed.

*

—How does one know when these things begin? Freddy says.

—I understand, she says.

—Gradually, Freddy says, what had seemed charming starts to become annoying, what had seemed like a quaint eccentricity becomes a source of constant irritation. Then, before you know where you are you're snarling at each other the whole time.

—I'm sorry, she says.

—Or, what's worse, he says, making a heroic effort to be polite to each other.

—Fortunately Giles and I found out we were incompatible within six months of being married, she says.

—I don't know, he says. We had some good times.

—Please! she says.

He laughs.

—You understand?

—Of course, he says. You're quite right.

—What are you doing? she says.

—Getting dressed.

—Already?

—I told you, he says. She's had this shock. Her best friend was killed standing on the platform of a bus.

—Yes, she says. You told me the first time we met.

—She needs support, he says.

—Of course, she says.

—It's different, he says, if someone's been ill for a long time. Then you can prepare yourself for it somehow.

—When will I see you?

—Would tomorrow be soon enough?

—It couldn't be too soon, she says.

—Same time?

—Same time.

—When did you begin to feel tired? the man asks.
—I don't know, Licia says. I feel as though I've been tired all my life.
—But you know that isn't true.
—I know, she says.
He perches at one end of the bench, looking out over the Common.
—I try to remember what it was like before, she says. But I can't. Not really.
—It came on you all of a sudden?
—I can't remember, she says. I had a bad cold and then I couldn't seem to get my energy back.
—Is it just physical? he asks. Or mental too?
—I don't know, she says. How can you distinguish?
He is silent.
—I just didn't want to work any more, she says. I just couldn't see the point.
—You must have seen the point once.
—Oh, I was very enthusiastic, she says. I was a very hard worker.
He is silent.
—It seems a long time ago, she says.
—You might wake up tomorrow and feel just like you once did, he says.
—Yes, she says.
—But you don't believe it.
—No, she says.
—We all need to stop once in a while, he says. To take a breather.
—Yes, she says.
—We can't just go on in the same old grooves.
—My father doesn't like it, she says.
—Your father?
—He doesn't like it.
—And it bothers you?
—I'd like him to understand.
—That's important for you?

She thinks about it.
—Is it? he says.
—Yes, she says.
—Why?
—He's my father.
—Perhaps, he says, he takes it as a personal affront.
—He does, she says.
—That's how it is with fathers.
—No, she says. You don't understand.
—I understand, he says.
—No, she says.
She stands up.
—I have to go, she says.
—You always stand up so abruptly, he says. As though if you didn't you'd never move.
—Really? she says.
—Yes.
—Well I must go anyway. Goodbye.
He bows to her but does not get up.

*

—No, Julie says. He's not back yet.
—Where is he?
—You must ask him that, Julie says.
—Julie, Ella says. Are you all right?
—I'm fine, Ella, Julie says. Fine.
—Your voice sounds funny.
—I'm fine.
—Are you sure?
—I'm fine, Ella.
—You wouldn't like to come round?
—Round? What for?
—I don't know. A chat. A cup of tea.
—No no. I'm fine. Really.
—He didn't say when he'd be in?
—No Ella.
—And you've no idea where he is?
—No.
—Can you get him to call me when he gets in?
—*Whenever* he gets in?
—What do you mean whenever?
—I mean, Ella, even if it's at two in the morning?
—He's only getting in at two in the morning?

—I don't know, Ella, Julie says. I don't know when he's going to get in.
—If it's after eleven tell him to ring tomorrow.
—I may not see him, Julie says. I may be asleep.
—Julie, Ella says, what are you talking about?
—I'm talking about Freddy. I need my sleep too, she says. I actually have to go to work tomorrow.
—You mean he might come in after you've gone to sleep and sleep on till after you've left?
—He might, Ella.
—I didn't realise, Ella says.
—Realise what?
—But if he comes in soon get him to call me, Ella says. All right?
—I will, Ella, Julie says. I will.
—Julie, Ella says, you're sure everything's all right?
—What could be wrong? Julie says.
—I don't know, Ella says. You sound funny.
—No, Ella, Julie says. It's your imagination. To myself I don't sound funny at all.
—Are you sure, Julie?
—What do you mean am I sure?
—Your voice sounds funny.
—I'm quite sure, Ella.
—That's all right then, Ella says. Goodnight dear. And don't forget to give him the message.
—If I see him, Julie says.
—Otherwise I'll call again tomorrow.
—Goodbye, Ella.
—Goodnight, Julie.
Ella puts down the phone. —He's not in, she says to her husband.
—So I gathered, Sam says.
—She sounded funny.
—So I gathered.
—She kept saying Ella all the time.
—Ella?
—She said he might not be in till two.
—Two in the morning?
—That's what she said.
—Nancy's death has upset her.
—What's he doing till two in the morning? she says.
—She didn't say?
—She just said he mightn't be in till two in the morning.
—Perhaps he needs to get out of the house.

64

—Do you think I should go round and see her?
—No, he says.
—You don't think so?
—No, he says.
—Not now, she says. I mean tomorrow.
—Oh, he says. I thought you meant now.
—I think I will, she says. You can't really tell on the phone, can you?

—I want to know how you are.
—I'm fine.
—Really?
—Yes of course.
—I just wanted to know.
—Now you know.
—Can I see you some time Liss?
—I'm very busy at the moment.
—Busy?
—Yes.
—I thought you weren't doing anything at the moment?
—Did you?
—I just thought . . . Is there some time we could meet?
—I don't think there is, Robin.
—I saw Freddy the other day, he says. He said you were fine.
—Yes I am.
—That's good. I was worried.
—Worried?
—I've been trying to get hold of you. Your mother told you I'm sure.
—Yes.
—She passed on my message?
—Yes.
—I asked you to call me.
—I've been very busy.
—What is it you're doing, Liss?
—Various things.
—You don't want to say?
—No.
—It's going well?
—Fine.
—No chance of seeing you?
—I don't think so, no.
—Not for a quick coffee or something?
—I don't think so.

—I really would like to talk to you.
—You're talking to me.
—I mean face to face.
—I'm sorry. I'm very busy.
—You won't tell me what you're doing?
—No.
—I see.
—Is that all then?
—I just wanted to find out how you were.
—I'm fine.
—That's good.
—'Bye then.
—'Bye Liss. And —if you change your mind. About having coffee or something . . .
—Sure.
—You've got my number.
—Yes Robin.
—Well. Goodbye then.
—Goodbye.

*

Freddy walks on the Common with his sister.
—She understands the children so well, Freddy says.
—Oh yes.
—You sound sceptical.
—You said the same thing about Petra.
—That was different.
—Oh?
—With Ness it's something instinctive, Freddy says.
—You said that's what drew you to Petra in the first place, Licia says.
—I did?
—Her instinctive affinity with the children.
—I can't have said that, Freddy says. Petra wasn't interested in children at all.
—I see.
—It's made a big difference to me, Freddy says. You don't know how tough the past few weeks have been at home.
—Why?
—The accident didn't help, he says. I tried to respond but I felt like a hypocrite the whole time. I wasn't particularly fond of Nancy.
—I know.
—You see what a position that put me in, he says.

—Yes, she says.

—But even without that, he says. Everything feels false. Even if a conversation starts out being natural it's as though we both suddenly become self-conscious about it, but just carry on, pretending we haven't noticed.

—You can't expect her to applaud.

—Applaud what?

—Your taking up with Ness.

—I'm not taking up with Ness.

—What are you doing then?

—It's not like that, he says.

They sit on a bench.

—I'd much rather we had a row, he says.

—Yes, she says.

—I don't really want to talk about it.

—I thought you did.

—No I don't. How's Simon?

—No change, she says. They won't discharge him till they're sure he won't have another and the more they keep him in the more desperate he gets. Ella bears the brunt of it as usual.

—You've been?

—No.

—Nor me, he says. I've been trying to write that catalogue intro. for Tony.

—I haven't any excuse.

—I didn't mean that.

—I can't seem to be able to get on tubes and buses these days, she says.

—It's as bad as that?

—There's nothing particularly bad. I just can't seem to get on tubes and buses, that's all. I can walk out here and sit on a bench and look at the sky. That's fine. Then walk home. That's fine too. And sit in a chair. Can't read. Can't think. Can't write. Can't really talk.

—You're talking now.

—I can with you.

—Not to Sam or Ella?

—No.

—Why don't you move out? I could find you something.

—I couldn't.

—Why not?

—I couldn't make the effort. And then I'm happy to let Ella feed me.

—I know what you mean. But if you made the effort . . .?

—I don't know how to make an effort any more, she says. When I think of what any effort might entail I panic. I don't know which part of myself I have to start galvanising first. It's as if the present moment is all I can cope with and as soon as I start to think about doing something different in the future it gets too much for me. That's not normal, is it?

—What does the doctor say?

—Same as you.

—Make an effort?

—Yes.

—Shit.

—Exactly.

—Why not try another?

—I've tried.

—Yes. You told me. I just thought one more . . .

—I'm too tired, she says. When I've been at table ten minutes I start to have difficulty keeping my head upright.

—I haven't noticed anything.

—It's all right when I'm outside. Or talking. But just sitting eating it's as if my head suddenly gets too heavy for my neck, or my neck too weak to hold up my head.

—Perhaps it's Sam.

—He contributes.

—He won't change.

—I know, she says.

—If I could get this intro. done, he says after a while, I might be able to see more clearly. But as long as it's hanging over me . . .

—See more clearly about what?

—Everything.

—You know that's not true, she says.

—Why not?

—There'd just be another intro.

—Yes, he says. I suppose you're right.

—There always is, she says.

—I'd like you to meet Ness, he says.

—Oh?

—I think you'd get on.

—Why?

—I think you'd respond to her warmth. I'd like her to meet you.

—Oh no, she says.

—I would. She's very interested in photography.

—I can't remember anything about photography any more.

—Bollocks.
—It's dead, she says. As far as I'm concerned photography is dead.
—Don't say that.
—It's true.
—For good, you think?
—Yes.
—Fair enough, he says.

*

—We're just off to the pool, Julie says.
—I won't keep you, Ella says.
—We're late already, Julie says. We were just hunting for the bathing suits.
—Don't let them stay in too long, Ella says.
—It won't hurt them, Julie says.
—That chlorine isn't good for the eyes, Ella says.
—It won't hurt them, Julie says. Not at their age.
—Does age make a difference? Ella asks.
Julie looks at her watch.
—I brought you this, Ella says. She hands her a plastic bag.
Julie looks inside. —Oh, she says. Thank you.
—To charge it you just leave it in its stand and plug it in, Ella says. You can leave it plugged in when you're not using it. It switches off automatically when it's charged up.
Julie goes to the well of the staircase and shouts: —Becky! Joe!
She comes back to the front door.
—Sam uses it to get the breadcrumbs off the table, Ella says.
—Thanks, Julie says.
—But it'll do the car as well, Ella says.
Julie looks at her watch.
—I hoped to have a word with you, Ella says.
—We're late as it is, Julie says.
—I thought your voice last night . . . Ella says. On the phone . . . I just wondered if . . .
The children came running down the stairs.
—Hallo darlings, Ella says.
—Go on, Julie says. Get into the car. We're late as it is.
—Hallo Granny.
—Hallo Granny.
—Go on, Julie says. Thanks for this, she says to Ella. You'll forgive us, won't you? We're late as it is.
—Just plug it in, Ella says. It switches itself off automatically when it's charged.

—She's not in, Sam says.
—I just wanted to know how she was, Robin says.
Sam holds the receiver and gazes out into the room.
—How is she? Robin asks after a while.
—Same as usual, Sam says.
—I'm sorry, Robin says.
—Why?
—I'm sorry she's not any better.
—There's nothing wrong with her, Sam says.
—I thought she was depressed.
—She's not depressed, Sam says.
—She's not?
—No.
—I'm so glad, Robin says.
Sam moves his tongue over his teeth, feeling out for any bits of food that might have got stuck there.
—Will you tell her? Robin says.
—Tell her what?
—I rang to see how she was.
—If I remember, Sam says.
—Yes of course.
—Is that all?
—Yes.
Sam puts the phone down. —It's that lunatic, he says to his wife.
—Who?
—Robin Iles.
—He's not a lunatic.
—He doesn't make sense.
—I hope you weren't rude to him.
—Me?
—You sounded rude.
—Me?
—He's always so polite, she says.
—I didn't think, he says, that at twenty-eight my daughter would still be getting phone calls from men she has no wish to speak to.

—You should try and be nice to him, she says. There's no reason to be rude.

—My great-grandmother was a grandmother at twenty-eight, he says.

—They married young then.

—How much longer is it going to go on? He says. That's what I want to know. How much longer?

—Try to be patient with her, Ella says.

—Patient? he says. You ask me to be patient?

—It's not her fault, she says.

—Whose fault is it then? he asks. Mine?

*

—Will you have another? Julie asks her sister.

—No thanks.

—I think I will, Julie says.

—Are you sure you should?

—Why the hell not?

—I just asked, her sister says.

—Why?

—You know why.

—Tell me.

—It sounded as though you were trying to punish yourself.

—Eating another doughnut is punishing myself?

—You know what I mean, Jule.

—Julie gets up and goes to the counter. She returns with a doughnut. She eats it in silence.

—I don't see why I shouldn't if I want to, she says.

Her sister sips her coffee, looking at her over the rim of the cup.

—There, Julie says, pushing the plate away. That's better, she says. She wipes her lips with a paper napkin.

—I don't see why I shouldn't if I want to, she says.

—Forget it, her sister says.

—Forget what?

—Forget I ever said anything.

—What did you say?

—It's not like you, her sister says.

—What's not like me?

—Letting yourself go like this.

—I'm letting myself go?

Her sister glances at her watch.

Julie stretches a hand out across the table and takes her arm.

—You're not going? she says.

—I've got to.

—Not before you've told me what you're trying to say.
—You know what I'm trying to say.
—No, Julie says.
Her sister stands up.
—You won't talk to me? Julie says.
—Oh come on, her sister says.
—You won't even deign to talk to me?
—Come *on*! her sister says.
—All right, Julie says. Let it go.
—I've got some things to pick up, her sister says.
—Of course.
—And you?
—What do you mean?
—Are you staying?
—I think I'll have another coffee.
—Fair enough, her sister says.
—I'm in no hurry, Julie says. I've got all day.
—'Bye then, her sister says.
Julie waves vaguely in her direction.
—'Bye, her sister says again.

*

—It's the smell of these places I can't stand, Simon says. The smell of staleness. Of age.
—I don't smell anything, Freddy says.
—You don't?
—No.
—You would if you were cooped up here night and day knowing you were never going to get out, Simon says.
—You'll be out in a few days, Freddy says.
—Never, Simon says.
—Don't say that.
—Never, Simon says again. I'll never get out of here alive.
—Of course you will, Freddy says.
—I tell you never.
Freddy looks round the ward.
—It's your mother, Simon says. She's *consigned* me to this for the rest of my days.
—What are you talking about? Freddy says.
—She's signed a piece of paper, Simon says. She's *abrogated* responsibility.
—I've talked to the doctor, Freddy says. If you go on progressing at this rate you'll be out of here by the end of the week.

—That's what they say to *you*, Simon says.
—Why should they lie to me?
The old man is silent, staring up at the ceiling.
—They want you out as much as we do, Freddy says. Don't think they don't.
—Feet first, Simon says. Feet first.
—Oh come off it, Freddy says.
—I can't fight them any more, Simon says. I don't have the strength to fight them any more.
—Why should you want to fight them? Freddy says. They're just as keen to see you healthy as you are.
—Do you know how many years it is since I was healthy? Simon asks him.
—How many?
—Fifty years, Simon says. That's what I've been celebrating this year: fifty years of ill-health.
—You're the fittest octogenarian I know.
—That's a compliment?
—It's a fact.
—Which doctor did you talk to?
—I don't know his name. He's looking after you. Indian I think.
—You don't even know his name? You say you care for me and you can't even be bothered to find out the name of the doctor dealing with me?
—I'm sorry.
—That's what I mean.
—What's his name then?
—Nasseem. Dr Nasseem.
—Right. Nasseem.
—En, ay –
—I know how to spell it, Freddy says.
—You're sure?
—You're looking a lot better than I expected, Freddy says.
—What did your mother say? A corpse?
—A corpse?
—Is that what she said?
—I gather you've been putting on weight too.
—Who told you that?
—The doctor.
—Nasseem?
—If you say so.
—You can't smell the stench of putrefaction? the old man asks him.

—No.
—The stale air of decay?
—No.
—She signed my death-warrant, he says.
—Oh come on.
—That's what it is. You've got to face the facts.
—I've got to go now, Freddy says.
—Of course.
—I'll see you at home next week.
—Don't joke about these things.
—Who's joking? You'll be home by the end of the week.
—Under the earth.
—I'm glad your spirits are so high.
—Never been higher.
—Cheerio then.
—Cheerio, dear boy.

—Are you going to read to me tonight?
—No. Mummy's reading to you tonight.
—Why not you?
—Because I have to go out.
—Where are you going?
—To work.
—Why don't you read to me before you go to work?
—Because it's Mummy's turn.
—I don't like the way she reads.
—Don't say that.
—She puts on a funny voice when she reads.
—I told you not to say that.
—He says it to annoy, Becky says.
—Don't you start, Freddy says.
—He does.
—That's enough from both of you.
—What are you going to do tonight?
—I told you: work.
—What sort of work?
—You know what sort of work.
—Looking at pictures?
—Yes.
—You call that work?
—I have to write about them afterwards.
—He's an art critic.
—I know.
—Then why do you ask?
—Because.
—You don't know what an art critic is.
—Yes I do.
—What is it then?
—Will you read to me tomorrow?
—What is it then?
—Leave him alone.
—When is Mummy coming home?

—Soon.
—Will you read to me tomorrow?
—Yes.
—About the fisherman and his wife?
—Yes.
—She's late, Becky says.
—Come on, Freddy says. Eat up your dinner.
—I don't want any more.
—Don't be tiresome.
—There she is.
—She's late, the little girl says.

*

—I finally got hold of her, Robin says.
—Oh yes?
—How is she?
—I thought you'd got hold of her?
—We just talked on the phone.
—Didn't she say how she was?
—She said she was fine.
—Then she's fine.
—How do you find her?
—Fine.
—So she's fine?
—Uhuh.
—She said she was fine.
—Yes, Freddy says. She's fine.
—She's not seeing anyone though?
—How do you mean not seeing anyone?
—Keeping to herself.
—Is she?
—I think so, yes.
—Ah.
—You don't see much of her yourself?
—No.
—I thought you were very close.
—We are.
—But you don't see much of her.
—No.
—I thought you saw a lot of each other.
—No.
—How is that?
—We're both so busy.

—She's very busy, is she?
—I think so, yes.
—What's she doing then?
—I don't know. She's always busy.
—She sounded low, Robin says.
—Did she?
—*I* thought so.
—From the way she spoke?
—Yes, and . . .
—And what?
—She seemed awfully defensive, Robin says.
—No no, Freddy says. You're imagining things.
—Am I?
—Yes.
—Do you think perhaps if I dropped round one of these days?
—No. I don't think that's a good idea.
—You think she needs time to sort things out?
—Sort things out?
—In peace and quiet I mean.
—I wouldn't call round like that, Freddy says. Not without her asking you I mean.
—Even if it was just for a moment?
—I don't think it's a good idea.
—No, I suppose not.
—I'm sure she'll be in touch. When she wants to see you.
—You think so?
—Yes. I think so.
—I had the feeling she didn't want to be disturbed, Robin says. But then I thought perhaps she'd like to be taken out of herself, sort of.
—No, Freddy says. I don't think she'd like that.
—I thought perhaps she didn't realise that what she needed was a bit of company. An evening out. Something like that.
—You asked her?
—I didn't quite get round to it. I wasn't sure . . .
—No, Freddy says. I'm sure if she'd wanted that she'd have suggested it herself.
—I thought perhaps she didn't quite realise . . .
—No, Freddy says. I don't think that's a good idea.
—I wasn't sure myself, Robin says. That's why I didn't . . .
—No, Freddy says.
—No what?
—I'm sure you did the right thing.

—In not pressing her?
—That's right.
—I thought so myself but I just wanted to check with you. After all you . . .
—No, Freddy says. I'm sure you did the right thing.
—I'm glad, Robin says.
—I'm sure you did.
—I'm glad.

*

—I didn't want to frighten you, Ella says.
—Frighten me?
—I thought you might be home very late, she says. I didn't want to frighten you.
—Why frighten? he says.
—Not with all the problems you've got at the moment, she says.
—What problems?
—You know what problems.
—I don't know what you're talking about, Freddy says. What was it you wanted to say?
—It's about Simon, she says.
—Simon?
—It's all right, she says. The doctors say he's stable at the moment. But you know how they are.
—What do you mean? he says. What's happened?
—You know how he is, she says.
—What do you mean, how he is?
—He kept grumbling they were keeping him there by force, she says. Then in the middle of the night he just got up and tried to sneak out.
—Tried to sneak out?
—He managed to evade the ward sister, she says, and get down the stairs, then another nurse intercepted him and asked him what he was doing. He told her he was on his way home and she tried to restrain him. He was in his pyjamas you see and she was suspicious. So they had a scuffle and she fell over and –
—Simon knocked a nurse over?
—She was trying to get him back upstairs and he panicked. She –
—He hurt her?
—Not badly, no.
—He's crazy.
—He panicked, she says. It's natural. He wanted to get away from the place. He thought they were keeping him there in spite of the

fact that he was perfectly well. He thought they wanted to keep him there till he died.

—He knocked over a nurse?

—Well, they struggled as he was getting out of the lift. They had gone back up in the lift together you see. She tried to get him out and they had a scuffle. He was only defending himself.

—He's a homicidal maniac.

—He was confused, she says.

—What happened?

—Well, as she fell she called out and a male nurse came to her help. He grabbed Simon and when Simon hit him he put his –

—He took on the entire hospital?

—He wanted to get out before it was too late, she says.

—What happened?

—I don't know, she says. He put his arm round his neck and –

—Who did? Who put whose arm round whose neck?

—The nurse. The male nurse. He was trying to restrain him. Simon had hit him in the face and his nose was bleeding.

—The nurse?

—Yes. So they –

—Oh my God! Freddy says.

—Then somehow he collapsed and –

—Who did?

—Simon. He suddenly collapsed and passed out. The hospital says it was his fault entirely. He had got over-excited.

—And so?

—They got him back to his bed but he didn't recover consciousness. They're denying all responsibility.

—He's *dead*?

—No no. He came to after a while. But it seems to have done something to his speech.

—He had a stroke?

—They're not saying what happened. Only that it's his fault.

—Of course it's his fault.

—They hope in time everything will get back to normal.

—You've seen him?

—I've just got back. He'd be so happy if you could get out there to see him.

—But I saw him last week.

—It wasn't necessary last week.

—What do you mean it wasn't necessary? You begged me to go out to see him. It took up a whole day.

—It would make me so happy.

—He can't stand the sight of me.
—Of course he can, she says. You know you're his favourite.
—He doesn't have any favourites. Except himself.
—Please, Freddy.
—If he's recovering he needs to be left in peace.
—Liss's going.
—You're forcing everyone to go?
—I'm not forcing anyone. How can you say that?
—I don't know.
—He hasn't got anyone in the world, she says.
—He has you.
—Please, Freddy.
—He's alienated everyone else with his selfishness.
—Please.
—You say he's on the mend?
—He's still looking a lot worse than he was last week.
—But he's still on the mend?
—That's what the hospital says. I don't think they know. He didn't look good to me.
—You think he's dying?
—I don't know, she says. I feel he's lost the will to live.
—I'd take their word for it. They know.
—It's in their interest to play it down, she says. They're afraid we'll sue.
—I should have thought they'd sue him, he says. It sounds as if he's committed every offence in the book.
—He was frightened, she says. He wanted to get home.
—So he knocked over a nurse and hit another one in the face?
—He didn't know what he was doing, she says. He was frightened.
—Can he talk?
—A little. It wasn't very clear.
—What did he say?
—He just mumbled he was done for, she says. I couldn't bear it.
—Sam's seen him?
—He came with me.
—What does he say?
—He doesn't think he'll last much longer.
—He agrees with you?
—If you saw him, she says.
—All right.
—Tomorrow if you can, she says. He may not last much longer.

—I've brought you your tea, Licia says.
—I hope you've brought yours as well, Nina says.
—I have.
—Then put it down on the table there and pour, will you?
—Do you want some of Ella's cake?
—Just a biscuit please, dear. Are you cold with the window open?
—No of course not.
—Have you been up to the Common today?
—Yes.
—Was it nice?
—Yes it was. Too hot.
—Yes, it's too hot for me. Even with a parasol.
—It's nice and cool here, Licia says.
—*I* like it, Nina says.
—Are you ready for another cup?
—Yes please.
—And another biscuit?
—No. I'm not hungry in this weather. Are you?
—No.
—What are you looking at?
—That photograph.
—It's one of yours.
—I know.
—Why are you looking at it?
—I don't know. I suddenly wanted to look at it.
—You gave it to me.
—You asked me for it.
—Yes. So I did.
—It's one of your trees.
—Yes.
—Do you remember where you took it?
—Yes.
—Where was that?
—Windsor Great Park.
—Ah yes. That's where it was.

—Will you have another cup?
—No thank you dear.
—That's what photography can do, Licia says. Remind you to look. Not at the photograph. The world.
She puts down her cup.
—Why are you staring at me like that?
—I'm just looking.
—What do you see?
—I don't know.
—That's right, Licia says. That's exactly right, Nina.
—Why?
—You know why.
—Yes dear. I do.

*

—How are things then? Freddy asks.
—Lousy, Simon says.
—You don't look too bad to me, Freddy says.
—I don't?
—You look rather well in fact.
—They say the dead are well, Simon says.
—Do they?
—Shakespeare. *Macbeth*.
—Really? *Macbeth*?
The old man lies on his back, his eyes closed.
—I hear you'll be out by the end of the week, Freddy says.
—Never, Simon says. Never.
—Oh come on.
—They'll see to that.
—I thought they'd put you in a room by yourself.
—You must be joking.
—They obviously don't consider you that dangerous.
—Me? Simon says. Dangerous?
—After all your exploits.
—What exploits?
—I hear you've been assaulting the nurses.
—My assaulting days are over.
—I hope so.
—Gone forever.
—I wish I could believe it.
—You want to see me dead?
—You mean you only feel alive when you're assaulting the nurses?
—I said that?

—You implied it.
 — I didn't assault any nurses.
 —I heard different.
 —You don't know what these people are like, Simon says. But I can't fight them any more. I give in. They've won.
 —You shouldn't have fought them in the first place.
 —I wanted to get home.
 —You were being irresponsible.
 —You don't know what this place is like. If you don't get out while you can you never will.
 —Rubbish. You'll be out by the end of the week.
 —We'll see about that.
 —You don't want to get out?
 —Of course I want to get out. But they won't let me. See if they do.
 —We'll see.
 —I was defending myself.
 —You took on the entire staff, so I gather.
 —I enjoyed it while it lasted, he says.
 —You enjoyed it?
 —I have to confess, yes.
 —Assaulting a defenceless woman? You enjoyed that?
 —Defenceless? Who's defenceless? I was in my pyjamas and slippers and they had their shiny uniforms and those great big boots, I can tell you it wasn't exactly an even match.
 —Still you did what you could. I just hope you don't assault any of them again.
 —I told you, he says. My assaulting days are over. They've seen to that.
 —When did they begin?
 —You came here to argue with me?
 —No no, Simon. I came to see how you were doing.
 —So now you see.
 —I'm very pleased.
 —Pleased to see a corpse?
 —Pleased to see how well you're doing.
 —I never thought it of you, he says.
 —Thought what?
 —There's a name for it, he says.
 —For what?
 —Necrophiliac, that's the name.
 —Necrophiliac?
 —That's right. A lover of corpses. That's you.

Freddy stands up.
—You've got to go? Simon says. Already?
—I'm sorry.
—Don't worry. Thanks for the visit.
—I'll see you in your own flat, Freddy says.
—Necrophiliac, Simon says. I never thought I'd have a necrophiliac for a great-nephew.
—Life's full of surprises, Freddy says.
—You can say that again.
—'Bye, Simon.
—Goodbye, my dear.

—I didn't think I would see you any more, the man says.
—No, she says.
—I thought you had abandoned me.
She laughs.
—I missed you, he says.
She is silent.
—It's funny, he says. A few months ago I didn't even know you. I still don't. And when you stopped coming I missed you.
—Habit, she says.
—Perhaps, he says.
—My great-uncle almost died, she says.
—How old is he?
—Eighty-something.
—And he's recovered?
—For the time being.
—What happened?
—He had a mild stroke and was taken to hospital, she says.
—And now he's back home?
—He didn't like it there. He didn't think they should be keeping him. He assaulted a nurse.
—That shows he can't have been too ill.
—Yes, she says. I suppose it does.
—Not, I hope, seriously.
—They decided to overlook it.
—You don't want to go to prison at that age, the man says.
—Oh, she says, I don't think it would have come to that. She tried to get him back to bed and he pushed her over.
—He's in the habit of doing that sort of thing?
—He's in the habit of getting his own way.
—Ah, he says. A dangerous habit.
She is silent.
—I thought perhaps you had taken yourself off to some other open spot, the man says.
—No no, she says. This is my Common.

—I was afraid my presence might have forced you to change your ways.

—No no, she says.

He is silent. Then he says: —He is by himself?

—Who?

—Your uncle.

—Great-uncle.

—Great-uncle.

—He prefers it that way, she says. He's lived like that since his wife died.

—No children?

—No. We're his nearest family.

—Quite a responsibility.

—My mother thrives on responsibility.

—Does she?

—Besides, he's independent enough. He's even what they call fiercely independent.

—I see.

—He comes to lunch most weeks.

—With you?

—With my parents.

—You live with your parents?

—For the time being.

—It suits you?

—Yes, she says. It suits me.

*

—I don't mind who you see, Julie says, but I won't have you bringing the children into it.

—What are you talking about? Freddy says.

—You know what I'm talking about, Julie says.

—My dear Julie, he says, I don't –

—Stop it, she says. You heard what I said.

—Heard what you said? I don't know what you're talking about.

—Yes you do, she says. I will not have you bringing your girlfriends on outings with the children.

—The children like her.

—I don't care.

—She likes them.

—You know what I mean, she says. If you take out the children it's you who takes them out, not you and someone else.

—I'm lonely. If you won't come out with us I need to have a companion.

—I have to work.
—That's what I'm saying.
—I'm telling you, she says. I won't have it.
—Why?
—Because I don't like it.
—If you would condescend to meet her you'd see how silly what you're saying is.
—I don't want to meet her.
—Fair enough.
—And I don't want her seeing the children.
—And I don't have a say in that?
—No.
—Why?
—You've forfeited your right.
—According to you.
—Precisely.
—You don't think you're being unreasonable?
—No.
—Well I do.
—That's too bad, isn't it?
—I suppose it is.
—I don't want it to happen again.
—And if it does?
—Just try it, she says. Just you try it and see.
—Perhaps I will, he says.

*

—Just here, Ella says. Just here above my breast.
—Here?
—Just here.
—And what exactly do you feel? Sam asks.
—A sort of pain, she says. A sort of sharp pain.
—It could be indigestion.
—Indigestion? In the heart?
—It only feels like the heart.
—If you had it you wouldn't say that.
—You've been running around too much, he says. You've been getting into a state about Simon.
—That's what's brought it on, she says. Just here, she says again, guiding his hand.
—Go and lie down.
—It's worse when I lie down.
—Then keep standing.

—Do you think I should see the doctor?
—Why not?
—But do you?
—Why not? If it sets your mind at rest.
—But they're so dismissive, she says. They never have any time for you.
—Do you know why that is? he says. It's because too many people come to them with imaginary ailments.
—Some aren't, she says.
—But most are.
—They should still find time for them, she says. Nobody *thinks* what they have is imaginary.
—What do you want to do then?
—I don't know, she says.
—It'll pass, he says. You probably ate too fast.
—I've had it before.
—Why didn't you say?
—I thought it would pass.
—You probably ate too fast.
—I was never a fast eater.
—Things change as one ages.
—It used to come and go, she says. Now I seem to have it all the time.
—Then go and see the doctor.
—But he won't even listen.
—Then try to forget about it.
—I can't, she says. It hurts.
—Perhaps he'll give you something for it.
—Like what?
—How should I know? If I knew I'd be a doctor.
—I think I'll give it one more day, she says. What are you doing?
—Making some tea.
—I'll do it. I said I'd do it.
—But you're not.
—I'm sorry.
—Let me do it.
—No no. Let me.
—All right, he says. But do it then.
—Yes, she says. I'll give it one more day.

*

—No, Licia says.
—Just a quiet meal, Robin says.

—No, Licia says.
—I can't come and see you for a few minutes?
—No.
—Are you all right Liss? he says.
—Yes yes, she says. Perfectly all right.
—You sound funny.
—Oh?
—You don't sound yourself.
—No no, she says. I'm myself all right.
—I saw Freddy the other day, he says. He said you were pretty low.
—He did?
—That's what he implied.
—I'll have to talk to him, she says. He has no right giving misleading information.
—I may have misunderstood him.
—Yes, she says. You must have misunderstood him.
—I gather you've been having family problems.
—I don't want to talk about it.
—I'm sorry.
She is silent.
—I don't want to be a nuisance Liss, he says. I just wanted you to know you could count on me.
—Whatever for?
—Anything, he says. Anything at all.
—I'll bear that in mind, she says.
—I'd like to be able to help, Liss, he says.
—I don't need help.
—No no. Of course. But if you do. I want you to know you can count on me.
—Thank you, she says.
—I mean it.
She is silent.
—Liss, he says.
—Yes?
—I want you to feel you can always speak frankly to me, he says.
—I know, she says.
—Tell me if I'm being a nuisance.
—Yes.
—I mean it, Liss.
—I know.
—You don't want to talk to me?
—Not at the moment, no.

—I see.
She is silent.
—Well, goodbye then, he says.
—Goodbye.

—Are you going out? Ella says to her mother. In this weather?
—When did I ever let the weather put me off?
—It's pouring with rain.
—I've got my umbrella.
—I'm going shopping in a minute, Ella says. If you'll just tell me what you need . . .?
—I'm going up to the Common.
—To the Common? In this weather?
—I've got my umbrella.
—Do you realise how hard it's raining?
—How often do I have to tell you? Nina says. In England you never wait upon the weather or you'll never get anything done.
—She's gone out for a walk, Ella says to Sam. In this weather.
—If it amuses her.
—She keeps saying she's always done that sort of thing but it's just not true.
—It won't do her any harm.
—It could kill her.
—It would take more than that to kill her, Sam says.
—She just doesn't realise, Ella says. She thinks she's done things all her life when she only started doing them yesterday. And nothing I say will ever convince her.
—It's her life, Sam says.
—I should have stopped her, Ella says.
—Nobody stops her, Sam says.
—She just won't listen to reason.
—You can say that again, Sam says.
—Is Liss in her room?
—How should I know? Sam says.
—You don't think she's out on the Common too in this weather?
—I wouldn't put it past her.
—Perhaps she's gone to the library.
—She went yesterday.
—She may have finished the book.
—Finished it? he says. She doesn't even read any more.

—Perhaps she found she'd already read it. Or perhaps she read it through in the night.

—At least if she was reading, he says. All she does is sit with the book open in front of her. I've watched her, he says. She doesn't even pretend to read. She doesn't even turn the pages.

—Why should she pretend? Ella says. In front of us.

—She doesn't even try, he says.

—She's tired, Ella says. Reading tires her.

—I'm the one who's tired, he says. I'm tired of that word tired. Do you understand?

—She can't help it.

—Then she should go to the doctor.

—She's been.

—And what did he find? Sam says. Nothing. All in the mind. Up there.

—I don't trust that man, she says.

—So? he says. She's been to other doctors. They all say the same. You don't trust any of them?

—How can they know? she says. They're not her.

—It's called medicine, he says. That's why they train for seven years. Precisely so they'll know. And what do they say? Unanimously? Nothing. Not a thing. Up there.

—She just needs a bit of peace and quiet, Ella says. She needs to think things through.

—That's not what she says, he says. She says she's tired. Full stop. What's that supposed to mean?

—I don't know, Ella says.

—God help me, he says. I don't know either.

—Patience, Ella says. Just a bit of patience. And then it'll sort itself out.

—A kick in the pants, Sam says. That's more likely to sort things out.

—Please, Sam, she says.

—You don't think I have her best interests at heart? he says. When have I ever had anything but her best interests at heart?

—Please, Sam, she says. Just give her time.

—How can I give what I don't have?

*

—But why? Nessa says.

—Because she doesn't like it.

—And me? Nessa says. I don't count?

—Of course you count, he says.

—It seems not, she says.
—You've got to see her point of view, Freddy says.
—And what's *your* point of view? she says.
—Please, Ness, he says.
—I was looking forward to it, she says.
—You've got to see her point of view, he says again.
—I *like* your children, she says. I *like* seeing them.
—I'm glad, he says.
—Then why not let me come with you?
—Because I promised Julie.
—They're your children too.
—That's not the point.
—It seems to me very much the point.
—I promised her, he says.
—But my question is why, she says.
—Because I can see her point of view.
—And you can't see mine?
—Of course I can.
—Well then.
—I don't think we should argue about it any more.
—You mean her point of view is more important than mine.
—I didn't say that.
—But that's what you're implying.
—Where the children are concerned, yes.
—But if they don't mind.
—That's the trouble, he says. It would be easy for her if they didn't like you. Surely you can see that.
—No, she says. I can't.
—What do you want me to do about it?
—Nothing now. But you might have thought of me when you promised her.
—It wouldn't be a problem if they didn't like you, he says again.
—I understand that, she says. I'm just asking where I come in your calculations, that's all.
—Please, Ness!
—Nowhere, she says.
—What?
—Isn't that the truth? Aren't you making it quite plain that that's precisely where I come in?
—You know that isn't true.
—But it is, she says. When it comes down to it that's the plain truth of the matter and I don't think I want to be there. Do you understand?
—Ness, he says.

—It's my fault, she says. I shouldn't have got into this in the first place.

—Yes, he says. It's your fault.

—That's all you have to say on the subject?

—If that's the line you want to take, he says.

—It's not the line I want to take, she says. It's the line you're forcing me to take.

—I'm not forcing anything, he says.

—Why don't you go back on your promise then? she says.

—Ness, he says.

—If you won't you won't, she says. But don't expect me to stand by and clap.

—I don't know how we got into this, he says.

—You know very well, she says. But you don't want to do anything about it.

He is silent.

—Do you? she says.

—No, he says.

—It smells, Simon says.
—I'll open the windows.
—It smells worse than the hospital.
—It'll be fine once I've got the windows open.
—At least there I'd begun to get used to it.
—You'll get used to this, Ella says. At least it's your flat.
—I feel like a ghost, he says. As if I've no right to be here any more.
—You'll be fine once we've settled you back in, she says.
—I bet you didn't expect me to return, he says.
—Don't be silly.
—I bet the neighbours didn't.
—You've only been away a fortnight.
—It feels like a lifetime, he says. What are you doing?
—Making you a cup of tea.
—A ghost, he says. As if I don't really have a right to be here. As if I've got in under the door.
—Stop making yourself ill, she says.
—I feel as if I'd died there and now I've just sneaked back to see the place for one last time.
—You'll be all right when you've had a good night's sleep, she says. Here's your tea.
—The furniture isn't expecting me, he says. It had resigned itself to a new life, new owners.
—Here. Have some tea.
—When you live in a place for a long time, he says, you stop seeing it. You just take it for granted. But when something like this happens to you, when you step back from the brink of death as I've done, then you realise how strange it all is.
—You'll get into the habit of it in no time, she says.
—I doubt it, he says. Not now I've seen it all looking so strange, so . . . temporary.
—Drink your tea before it gets cold, she says.
—It might have been better to have made a clean break, he says.

—When you were there all you wanted to do was get back here, she says. And now you're complaining.

—I'm not complaining, he says. You always confuse everything. I'm just stating a fact.

—The smell's gone already, she says. It's just because everything was shut for a few days.

—When I lie down on my bed, he says, I'll be thinking: It didn't expect to have me lying on it ever again. It had already forgotten me. I shouldn't be doing this to it.

—Don't work yourself up, she says.

—When I sit down on my chair, he says, I'll feel like an intruder. As if I shouldn't be doing that. As if I'm desecrating the place by being there at all.

—You're getting yourself into a state, she says. Remember how you longed for this when you were there.

—It's too late now, he says.

—It isn't too late.

—It is, Ella.

—Didn't you beg me to take you home? Didn't you shout at me because you thought I was forcing you to stay?

—That's true, he says. But it doesn't alter the facts. I went too far, he says. I went too far over to the other side.

—No you didn't, she says.

—There are some doors, he says, when you open them, it's never the same again.

—Do you want another cup of tea?

He holds out his cup. —Never the same again, he says again.

—You'll never settle back in if you take that attitude, she says.

—I'm just facing the facts, Ella.

—I'll have to go soon, she says. Will you be all right, do you think?

—It depends on what you mean by all right.

—I've stocked up the fridge, she says. I think you've got everything you want.

—It depends on what you mean by all right, he says again.

—I'll call you this evening, she says.

—The ghost will answer.

—Good.

—Its voice will be my voice.

—You're sure you've got all you want?

—Nobody ever has that, my dear.

—And I'll see you tomorrow.

—The ghost, he says. You'll see the ghost. He looks so much like me you won't be able to tell the difference. A little thinner, perhaps, a little more crumpled, but that can be put down to age, to the shock of what's happened.

—Good, she says. Then I'll see you tomorrow.

*

—I'm tired, she says.
—Where? her father asks.
—Everywhere.
—All the time? he asks.
—All the time, she says.
—If you made the effort it might help, he says.
—I can't, she says.
—She's an interesting person.
—I know.
—It's all set up, he says. A free trip. The publishers pay for it all.
—You don't understand what I'm telling you.
—You'd be doing her a favour and, who knows, yourself as well.
—No, she says.
—It's just a few gardens, he says. You can do them in your sleep.
—I don't want to photograph any gardens.
—I went to a lot of trouble to set it up, he says.
She is silent.
—It wasn't easy, he says.
She is silent.
—You'll have an interesting time, he says. And, maybe, when you start the urge will come back.
—I don't want to start.
—There may not be another chance.
—I don't want another chance.
—She admires your work, he says.
—It's not my work.
—Whose is it then? he says. Mine?
—I told you not to bother, she says. I told you I wouldn't do it.
—She's counting on you, he says. The publisher's counting on you.
—I told you I wouldn't do it.
—Just to help her out of a hole.
—I don't want to help her.
—What do you want to do then?
—Nothing.
—Nothing you've been doing all this time, he says. Now's the moment to do something.

—I'm tired, she says. I'd do it if I wasn't so tired.

—Tell her, he says. Tell her to do it.

—If she's tired, Ella says.

—I'm fed up with hearing she's tired, he says. I get her this thing, out of the blue, a golden opportunity, and this is how she thanks me.

—I told you from the start, she says. I told you I didn't want to do it.

—So I've got to keep you till the day I die? he says.

—Sam, his wife says.

—She's twenty-eight, he says. A grown woman. And she acts like a twelve-year-old.

—She's tired, Ella says.

—Don't tell me she's tired! he suddenly screams. Don't use that word again. Do you understand?

They are silent.

—What do I tell her? he asks his daughter. What do I tell her after I said you would do it?

—I didn't say I would.

—I tell her you're too tired? I tell her a grown woman of twenty-eight is too *tired* to photograph a few gardens? You expect me to tell her that? How do you think that makes me look? Too tired to go on a paid-for holiday? Too tired to take a few photographs?

—Sam, his wife says.

—Well? he says. What do I tell her?

—You tell her it was a misunderstanding.

—A misunderstanding? After I told her you would do it?

—I never said I would.

—You didn't say you wouldn't.

—Yes I did. From the start.

—I didn't hear you.

—I've told you. I never want to take a photograph again.

—And can you tell me why?

—No.

—What's that supposed to mean?

—I don't know.

—In ten minutes she's going to ring up, he says. What am I supposed to tell her?

—Tell her I won't.

—And if she asks me why?

—Tell her the truth.

—And what's the truth?

—Tell her I'm tired. Tell her I'm not taking any more photographs.

—You want me to tell her that?
She is silent.
—I asked you a question, he says.
—Yes, she says. Tell her that.

—We would only see Mother twice a day, Nina says. Once in the middle of the morning and once when she came to kiss us goodnight. Sometimes she would take us out to tea with her.

—Golly, Julie says.

—That's the way it was, Nina says. Our real mother was Nanny. She brushed our hair and dressed us and took us out and read to us and undressed us and put us to bed.

—Did she and your mother get on? Julie asks.

—Up to a point, Nina says. Of course there was tension between them. Even we could sense that. But there was also mutual respect.

—It's hard to imagine, Julie says.

—A blip, Simon says to Freddy. I think of it as a blip and nothing more.

—Part of the rich tapestry of life, Freddy says.

—Exactly, Simon says. You take the words out of my mouth.

—More like a holiday really, Freddy says.

—You could put it like that, Simon says. Certainly I haven't felt better in a long while.

—Once upon a time, Sam says. I can never get beyond once upon a time.

—Yes you can, Joe says. If you try.

—Let me see, Sam says. What comes after once upon a time?

—There was a giant.

—A giant was there? And what did the giant do?

—He ate people.

—Ate them? Bones and all?

—He threw away the bones. They piled up in a heap in a corner of the house.

—But not before he'd gnawed them clean.

—What's nawd?

—Like that.

—Go on.

—Let's see then. Once upon a time there was a giant who ate people. He gnawed the bones clean and threw them in a heap in a corner of his house. And gradually the heap grew bigger and bigger.

—It made a noise.
—What made a noise?
—When he threw the next bone on the heap.
—You bet it did. A thudding noise. A tinkling noise. Right down through the whole pile of bones. Thud. Tinkle. Tinkle. Tinkle. Silence.
—Only the sound of him nawing and swallowing.
—Of course. There was no one else around so he didn't have to mind his table manners.
—He let the food dribble down his chin.
—Stain his pullover.
—Filthy his trousers.
—The smell in the house was disgusting, but the giant didn't notice because he was too busy eating.
—Don't pick at the icing, dear, Ella says.
—Can I have a slice now? Becky asks.
—If you promise not to tell anyone.
—I promise.
—Look, I'll cut it up like this so no one will notice and then you can have this small slice.
—Can I have this one?
—All right dear. But don't wipe your hands on your dress.
—Did you make it, Gran?
—Of course I did. Do you want me to teach you how?
—Yes please.
—You'll have to come round early next time and I'll show you.
—Mummy never makes cakes.
—Only grannies make cakes, Ella says.
—Why?
—Because that's how it is.
—Won't I be able to make a cake till I'm a granny?
—Grannies and little girls. Nobody else.
—Pam's mother makes cakes. They're not as good as yours.
—I'm only talking about good cakes. Only grannies and little girls make really good cakes.
—I never said that, Freddy said.
—I didn't think you had, Licia says.
—Why does he go around saying I did?
She shrugs.
—Thanks for telling me, he says. I'll have a word with him about it.
—Don't do that.
—I don't like people saying I said things I never said.

—He wanted to protect himself.
—He doesn't need to bring me into it.
She is silent.
—I told him to stop pestering you, he says.
—There was no need.
—I told him you had other things on your mind.
—Ella likes talking to him.
—Some people can't take a hint, Freddy says.
She shrugs.
—You're not going to do those gardens then? he asks after a while.
—No.
—It didn't tempt you?
—No.
—Fair enough.
—I wouldn't know how to begin.
—Oh come on!
—Not any more, she says.
—Fair enough, he says.
—They don't realise what it means to be tired, she says. It means you can't conceive of making the effort. It means you've forgotten everything you once knew. It means you know nothing and can do nothing.
—Fair enough, he says.
—You know what I mean?
—I believe you.
—When Nanny died, Nina says, we didn't even know how to brush our own hair. Twelve-year-olds and we didn't even know how to do that.
—Gracious, Julie says.
—That's what it was like in those days, Nina says.
—Not in my family it wasn't, Julie says.
—Yes, Nina says. That's what it was like. You weren't prepared for anything except to lead the life your mother and her mother had led before you.
—My, Julie says.
—There was one charming nurse, Simon says. Hair down to here. Eyes like stars. A gazelle.
—I didn't see her.
—Adorable, Simon says. I took her phone number.
—You've rung her?
—I'm waiting till I'm a little stronger.
—Don't wait too long.

—Came from Surinam. Hair like a waterfall.

—Pity she was never on duty when I came to see you.

—If you'd come more often I'd have introduced you. Not just beautiful either. Cultured. Her father was a professor of mathematics. An expert on string theory.

—And the more people he ate, Sam says, the more he wanted to eat.

—How many did he eat a day?

—That depended. Some days nobody called and so he didn't get a chance to eat anyone. On other days he ate so many people he was sick.

—Did he eat anything else besides people?

—No. He was a strict carnivore.

—What's a carnival?

—Someone who eats meat.

—And drinks blood?

—And drinks blood.

—Did he have any friends?

—No. He didn't have any friends and he didn't want to have any either. When he wasn't eating he slept. And when he wasn't sleeping and there were no people to eat he played with the bones.

—How did he play with them?

—He juggled with them. He juggled with the shinbones.

—What did he do?

—He sat cross-legged on the floor and he tossed them into the air six at a time, so that they made an arc over his head as he sat cross-legged on the floor of his room. He would juggle like that for hours at a time, always catching them and throwing them up again, to stop himself thinking about how hungry he was.

—And then he slept.

—Not when he was hungry. When he was hungry he couldn't sleep. He only slept when he'd had a good meal.

—No, Ella says, you can help me put the cakes on the table.

—Can I take this one?

—Put it on the table and then go and sit down.

—Can I come back and get another one?

—If you like.

—I'd like you to meet her, Freddy says.

—I don't know.

—I'm sure you'd like her.

—You always say that.

—That's true.

—Why are you so sure?

—I just am. She loves children.
—I don't.
—Yes you do.
—Only yours.
—So does she.
—And they?
—You know how it is with children. You can't tell what they're really thinking.
—*You* can't tell?
—I think they do, he says.
—Have some tea, Ella says.
—Thanks.
—And some cake.
—I'll have some of that one.
—Liss?
—Not for the moment thanks.
—Nina?
—What is it dear?
—Your tea.
—Oh, thank you.
—Have some cake.
—What are you giving the children? Julie asks her.
—I've got some of that mango drink they like.
—It's not too sweet?
—It's the brand they like.
—We're going to stop now, Sam says, and have some tea.
—I don't want any tea.
—You don't want any cake?
—I want you to go on with the story.
—I can't with my mouth full.
—When you've finished.
—Perhaps it's enough for one day.
—But you've only just begun!
—Have I?
—Yes.
—Well you go on then.
—I can't. You go on.
—We'll see after tea. I may get inspired.
—Can't you go on now?
—I'm not a giant. I can't speak with my mouth full.
—Then don't fill your mouth.
—But I've got to have my tea. Why don't you eat some of Granny's cake?

—If you promise to go on afterwards.
—We'll see.
—Promise!
—Never promise what you can't be sure of fulfilling.
—Why can't you be sure?
—Because I may have run out of inspiration.
—Fit as a fiddle, Simon says. Never felt better.
—You look well, Julie says.
—I feel well, Simon says.
—I haven't seen you looking so well in a long time, Julie says.
—You've got to be able to bounce back, Simon says. Resilience. That's the secret.
—You've certainly got it.
—Either you have it or you don't, Simon says. It's not something you can learn. I'm fortunate in that I've always had it.
—You're an example to us all.
—I wouldn't say that.
—I hope I have half your resilience when I'm your age.
—It's no use hoping, Simon says. It's innate. Either you've been born with it or you haven't.
—I don't think I've been born with it, Julie says.
—I've been in some pretty tight corners in my life, Simon says. But I've always managed to bounce right back.
—No, Sam says. I'm not taking him back.
—But he's only just come out of hospital.
—I'm not setting a precedent. If he wants to come here he can come on his own steam.
—But you did it before.
—To please you.
—Then please me again. Where are you going? Ella says to her mother.
—I'm just going to show Becky something.
—What?
—Something in my room.
—You want me to fetch it?
—No dear. We are just going up to see it. Just the two of us.
—Where's Joe? Julie asks her husband.
—I don't know, Freddy says. In the garden perhaps.
—We've got to start getting ready soon.
—Becky's just gone upstairs with Nina.
—Whatever for?
—She was going to show her something.
—Well find Joe. As soon as they come down we have to leave.

—Perhaps he's in the kitchen.
—Just find him, will you?
—I think I saw him go into the kitchen.
—I wish your mother wouldn't give them all that sugar, Julie says to Licia. It's rotting their teeth.
—Is it?
—Everybody knows sugar's bad for the teeth. Except your mother, it seems.
—They look healthy enough to me.
—Have you looked inside their mouths? Julie says.
—No, Licia says.
—It's not a pretty sight, Julie says. Believe me.
—I believe you, Licia says.

*

In the car Julie says, under her breath: —I've asked you before. Do not put your hand there.
—What are you talking about? Freddy says.
—I don't like it.
—I can't believe this, he says.
—I'm serious, she says. I'm warning you.
—Warning me?
—I won't be responsible for my actions, she says, if it happens again.
—You're not warning me, he says. You're threatening me.
In the back Becky nudges her brother: —Look what Nina gave me.
He stares out of the car window.
—Look, Becky says, look what Nina gave me.
—I don't want to look.
—All right. I was just doing it for you.
—It's not a joke, Julie says in the front.
—I can see that, Freddy says.
—No you can't.
—I can put my arm round your shoulders?
—I'm warning you, she says.
—This is preposterous, he says.
—Just try it.
—What exactly am I supposed to have done?
—It's your last chance, Becky says.
Her brother does not reply.
—What exactly am I supposed to have done? Freddy repeats.
—You want me to tell you?

—That's the idea.

—You put your hand there, she says, you propel me out of the room ahead of you with your hand *there*, and you think you're being *gracious*.

—Gracious?

—Son, husband, father, all in one, she says.

—That's gracious?

—You know what I'm talking about.

—I'm flabbergasted.

—Give it a little thought, she says. For once.

—You don't like the sensation of my hand on your waist?

—It's not my waist.

—For God's sake, he says. I'm not pinching your bum.

—You know what you're doing.

—You mean I'm flaunting my rights over you in public? Is that what you mean?

—You know what I mean, she says. And you know what will happen if you do it again.

—You'll turn round and slap me? Slap me? In front of my mother? My children? Perhaps you'll say something like: Take your greasy hands off my bum, you bastard?

—I'm warning you, she says.

—All right, Joe says in the back. Let me see.

—No.

—Please.

—It's too late. You had your chance.

—Please Beck!

—What if I forget? Freddy says.

—I'm just warning you.

—Yes. I heard you.

—That's clear then, she says.

—No, Becky says. You had your chance. Now it's too late.

—Of all the benches in London you could go and sit on and of all the benches in London I could go and sit on, he says, and this is the one we come to.
—Yes, she says.
—This is the one I always come to, he says, and it is the one you always come to.
—Yes, she says.
—Do you remember when you first started coming to this bench? he asks her.
—No, she says.
—Me neither, he says.
They sit.
—Perhaps you think of it as your bench, he says. Perhaps you resent my being here and wish I would move to another.
She is silent.
—Is that what you sometimes think? he asks.
—What?
—That you would like the bench to yourself. That you resent the fact that I too think of it as my own.
—No no, she says.
—Do you ever think, I wonder, he says, that I might be feeling the same thing? That I might be resenting the fact that you have made this bench your own when I feel that it is mine?
—Do I?
—But then I think, he says, why should I be the one to move? I like the view from here more than I do from any of the other benches, why should I give way to her?
She is silent.
—Do you think that too? he asks.
—Think what?
—That you don't see why you should be the one to move.
—To move?
—To find another bench. Another Common.
—No, she says.
—You don't sometimes think that?

—No.
—But now that I have mentioned it, he says, you don't think there is some truth in it?
—I don't know what you are talking about, she says.
—It was just a thought that crossed my mind, he says. As I sat here this morning.
After a while he says: —Would you prefer it if I didn't talk?
—I don't know, she says.
—I've thought of it, he says, but then I thought it would be a little funny, just the two of us on this bench, on this Common even, and we didn't speak. It wouldn't be natural, would it?
—No, she says.
—It was just a thought, he says.
She is silent.
—I was reading in the paper, he says, that the Government is thinking of banning remote controls on TV sets so as to make people get up if they want to switch channels. They feel it would help to keep the population healthy. Analysis has apparently shown, he says, that even the movement from the sofa to the TV set and back makes a big difference to a person's health.
—It wouldn't work, she says. People would smuggle them in.
—They could have vans going round checking, he says. Like for licences.
She is silent.
—It's a bit like cigarettes I suppose, he says. Or drugs. Do you decrease consumption by banning or would that only increase curiosity? My own view, he says, is that on balance banning works. It's simply easier not to smoke if they won't sell you cigarettes, or, presumably, to get up to switch channels if the only sets in the High Street are the kind that require you to do so.
She stands up.
—You have to go? he asks.
—Yes.
—I hope I haven't put you off with my talking?
—No.
—You're sure?
—Yes. I have to go.
—Goodbye then, he says.
—Goodbye.

*

—She's out at the moment, Ella says.
—Do you know when she'll be back?

—No, Ella says. Do you want to leave a message?
—It's not important, Robin says.
—She shouldn't be long, Ella says.
—She's working again?
—No, Ella says. She's still turning things over.
—Something came up I thought might interest her, Robin says.
—I don't think she wants to take on anything new at the moment, Ella says.
—It wouldn't require much work.
—I don't think she wants to take on anything at all.
—I just thought I'd mention it.
—It's very kind of you, Ella says. I'll pass on the message. But I don't think she wants to take anything on at present.
—Fair enough, Robin says.
—It's very kind of you, Ella says. And is your own work going well?
—So-so, Robin says.
—Only so-so?
—And you?
—Oh, we're fine.
—I hear your uncle's been poorly.
—It's all right. He's out of hospital now.
—I'm so glad. And your mother?
—She's fine.
—Good, Robin says. Good.
—I'll give her the message.
—If she's interested she can phone me, Robin says. She has my number.
—I'll tell her, Ella says.
—Tell her not to leave it too long.
—I'll tell her.
—Goodbye.
—Goodbye.

*

—'"Husband," said she, "go to the fish and tell it I want to be Emperor."
'"Ah, wife," said the man, "he can't make you Emperor. I can't ask for such a thing. There's only one Emperor at a time. The flounder can't make Emperors, he just can't do it."
'"What!" said the woman, "I'm King, and you're my subject. You go this very minute. If it can make Kings then it can make Emperors too. I want to be Emperor. Go!"

'Then he had to go. But as he went he grew frightened and thought to himself: "This just isn't right. Emperor is too much. The flounder's going to get tired of this."

'With that he came to the sea. The sea was all black and thick and began to boil up so that it bubbled and seethed and a great wind passed over it so that the water swirled and reared up as though it were alive, and the man was terrified. Then he went and stood by the shore and said:

> "Munntje munntje timper tee
> Flounder, flounder in the sea –
> My good wife, dame Ilsebill,
> Wills not what I'd have her will."

'"Well, what does she want then?" said the flounder.
'"Ah, flounder," said the man, "she wants to be Emperor."
'"Just go on home," said the flounder. "She's already Emperor."
'Then the man went back and when he got there the whole castle was made out of polished marble, with alabaster figures and golden ornaments. Soldiers were parading up and down in front of the gate, blowing on trumpets and beating on drums, and inside the house there were barons and counts and dukes, all hurrying back and forth as though they were servants. They opened the doors of solid gold for him, and when he went in there was his wife sitting on a throne that was made out of a single piece of gold two miles high and she had on a great golden crown at least three yards high, set with diamonds and carbuncles. And in – '

—Your mother, Julie says, standing in the doorway.
—What does she want?
—She seems to be in a state.
—But what is it?
—She's in a hurry to talk to you.
He puts the book down. —I'll be back in a moment, he says to his son.
He picks up the phone. —It's Nina, his mother says.
—What about her?
—I just went up to her room. She was . . .
—What? he says. What's the matter?
—She's dead.
—Oh my God, he says.
—She's dead, she says again.
—What happened?
—Please, she says. Just come.

—I'll be right over.
He puts down the phone. —Nina's dead, he says to Julie. Where are the keys?
—Nina? Julie says. What happened?
—I don't know, he says, heading for the door. I don't know.

—She died in her sleep, Licia says.
—There was nothing the matter with her?
—Just the usual small things. Nothing serious.
The man is silent.
—My mother went up to call her to dinner, Licia says, and she didn't reply. But as soon as she entered the room she knew she was dead.
—That's the best way, the man says.
—Yes, Licia says.
—It's the best way, he says again.
—My father was out that evening, she says. Luckily I was there.
—If she didn't suffer that's the best way, the man says.
—Yes, Licia says.
—Suffering before death is terrible, the man says. There is nothing you can do for the suffering person. They are lost to you long before they actually die. But you suffer with them. Uselessly.
—My brother came over right away, Licia says. We didn't know how to get hold of my father.
After a while the man says: —I thought it was your great-uncle you were worried about.
—Yes, Licia says. There was never anything wrong with Nina.
After a while the man says: —Do you want to talk about it?
—No, Licia says.
—I understand, he says.
—There's nothing to talk about.
—I understand.
She is silent.
—These things, he says, one never gets over them. Never.
—I don't want to get over it, she says.
—No, he says.
—Life goes on, she says.
He is silent.
—As you see, she says, here I am again.
—I thought you had moved on, the man says.

—No, Licia says.
—I understand, the man says.

*

—'Then he went and stood and had a good look at her,' Freddy read. 'And when he'd looked at her for a long time he said: "Ah, wife, how nice that you're Emperor."

'"Husband," she said, "what are you standing there for? Now that I'm Emperor I want to be Pope. Go on back to the flounder at once!"

'"Ah, wife," said the man, "is there anything you don't want? You can't be Pope. In all Christendom there's only one Pope. There's no way the flounder can make you that."

'"Husband," said she, "I want to be Pope. You go on back to the flounder this instant. I've got to be Pope today."

'"No, wife," said the man. "I don't want to ask him that. This will come to a bad end; it's asking too much. The flounder can't make you Pope."

'"Nonsense!" said the wife. "If it could make me Emperor it can make me Pope. I'm the Emperor and you're my subject, so just you go!"

'Then he was frightened and went, but he felt all faint, and he shivered and shook and his knees and the calves of his legs trembled. And the wind blew over the land, and the clouds scudded and it grew dark as night; the leaves fell off the trees, the waters surged and roared as though they were boiling, and the sea rose to the height of a steeple and crashed down on the shore, and far off in the distance you could just see ships firing off distress signals and dancing up and down on the waves. There was a tiny patch of blue in the middle of the sky but on the horizon it was as red as though a great thunderstorm were coming up. He went and stood by the shore, all timid and fearful, and said:

> "Munntje munntje timper tee
> Flounder, flounder in the sea –
> My good wife, dame Ilsebill,
> Wills not what I'd have her will."'

He closes the book.
—Go on, his son says.
—That's enough for tonight.
—But I'm not asleep yet.
—You should be.

—Oh, please! Just a bit more.
—You're very tired. You were almost asleep.
—I wasn't!
—That's enough. Now go to sleep like a good boy.
—Will you go on tomorrow?
—Yes.
—Promise?
—Yes.
—All right.
—Goodnight.
—Goodnight.

He enters the little girl's room. She is curled up in bed, holding her book half under the bedclothes.

He bends over and kisses her. —Will you go to sleep now? he says.
—All right.
—Put the book away.
—I'll just finish this bit.
—Up to where?
—Here.
—Promise?
—Yes.
—All right. Goodnight.
—Goodnight.

*

—Do you want to move into her room? Ella says to her daughter.
—Why?
—It's the nicest room in the house.
—I've got mine.
—I just thought you might like to.
—I couldn't, Licia says.
—I hoped you would.
—Why?
—I don't know. I wanted to feel it was inhabited.
—Then I will.
—Otherwise we'll never use it again.
—Why don't *you* move there?
—It's not big enough for two.
—All right, Licia says.
—Only if you'd like to.
—I'd rather not.
—Why don't you think about it?

116

—All right.
—I know she'd have liked that.
—I'll think about it.
—I only want you to do it if you feel you'd like to.
—At the moment I'd rather not.
—All right.
—You'll find a use for it.
—Yes, Ella says.
—I'm used to where I am.
—I know dear. I just thought . . .
—You'll find a use for it.
—Perhaps.

—What's her death got to do with it?
—Everything, he says.
—I don't understand, she says.
—That's too bad.
—What do you mean it's too bad?
He is silent.
—I'd understand if you said you couldn't see me for a while, she says. I'd understand that perfectly well. I'd expect it even. But to call it off . . .
He waits.
—Are you there? she says.
—Yes, he says.
—Well, say something.
He is silent.
—I said I'd understand if you didn't want to see me for a few weeks, she says. But what I can't understand is why it should lead to the end of us.
He waits.
—Can you explain? she asks.
—No, he says.
—You don't think you owe me an explanation?
He is silent.
—Don't you?
—No, he says.
—Is it anything I've done?
—No, he says.
She waits.
—Aren't you going to say anything? she asks.
He is silent.
—Well thank you very much, she says.
He waits.
She waits.
She puts down the phone.

*

—I'm sorry, Robin says.
—Thank you.
—I tried to get hold of you, he says. As soon as I heard. I spoke to Ella.
—I know, she says.
—I'm terribly sorry.
—Thank you.
—I'd like to come and see you, he says.
—I'd rather not.
—You'd rather I didn't?
—Yes.
—You're sure?
—Yes.
—Not straight away of course, he says.
She is silent.
—You're all right? he says.
—Yes.
—I understand, he says. I'll call again next week. I'd just like to see you.
—Thank you.
—Ella said she'd died in her sleep.
—Yes.
—That's a blessing.
—Yes.
—I thought of writing but it's so impersonal.
—Yes.
—Not that the phone's much better.
—No.
—I'll call again next week anyway. All right?
—Yes.
—Goodbye.
—Goodbye.

*

—She had a good life, Simon says.
—You think so? Sam says, his eyes on the road.
—Full, Simon says. Interesting. Surrounded by loved ones. What more can you ask?
—Ella feels she could have been less hard on her.
—Of course she does, Simon says. All children feel that when a parent dies. I felt that when my father died, may his soul rest in peace. What's happening?
—I don't know, Sam says.

—We don't usually get held up here, Simon says.
—They're probably doing something to the road.
—You didn't come this way on your way to me?
—It was clear then.
—Unbelievable, Simon says. Unbelievable.
—She feels she took her too much for granted, Sam says.
—Of course she did, Simon says. That's the only way to live with someone, isn't it?
—She feels she gave her time to all sorts of people who weren't nearly as close to her and somehow never bothered with her.
—I felt like that when my father died, Simon says.
—I know, Sam says.
—It's not as if one wasn't expecting it, Simon says.
—You were?
—At that age, Simon says, surely . . . ?
They begin to move again.
—I don't see any roadworks, Simon says.
—No, Sam says. I don't know what it was.
—Unbelievable, Simon says. Absolutely unbelievable.
—I don't think we ever thought . . . Sam says.
—You didn't?
—She seemed so healthy.
—You mean you never . . . ?
—Of course we knew that sooner or later . . .
They stop again.
—What is it now? Simon asks.
—I don't know.
—You don't think we're going to be late for lunch?
—They'll wait.
—I must say I'm beginning to feel quite peckish.
—Perhaps, Sam says, if you don't talk about it . . .
—She doesn't want it mentioned?
—If she brings it up of course . . .
—I understand.
—I'm sure you do.
—Sometimes, though, Simon says, it's better to have these things out in the open. Clear the air.
—It's been out in the open quite enough in the last three weeks, Sam says.
—I understand.
—There comes a point when it's perhaps better to refrain.
—A moratorium, Simon says.
—Exactly.

—I understand.

He looks at his watch: —Did it always take this long?

—It's a long way.

—You seemed to do it more quickly before.

—Some days are better than others.

—You'd have thought, Simon says, it would even itself out.

—On the contrary, Sam says. Either everything goes your way or nothing does.

—Like life, Simon says, and laughs.

Sam glances round at the old man. —Like life, he agrees.

Simon looks at his watch. —The tube is really much quicker, he says.

—Yes, Sam says.

—It's a pity my condition precludes my taking the tube, Simon says.

—Yes, Sam says. A great pity.

—I used to enjoy taking the tube, Simon says. You see a bit of life there.

—I used to enjoy Sunday mornings at home, Sam says.

—How things change.

—Yes, Sam says.

—At least it gives us a chance to natter, Simon says.

—Yes.

—I'll miss our little chats when I get back to taking the tube, Simon says. It's never the same with other people around, is it?

—No, Sam says.

—One needs the space, Simon says. The mental space. For a genuine exchange. In fact a car ride is the ideal environment for a really good natter, isn't it?

—Maybe, Sam says.

—Always the cautious one, Simon says, laughing. Always the cautious one.

—It's not caution, Sam says.

—I'm not criticising, Simon says. God forbid.

—No? Sam says.

—God forbid, Simon says. He looks at his watch. —Much longer? he asks.

—Who knows? Sam says.

—That's the trouble with cars, Simon says. You never know, do you? You're the victim of circumstances.

After a while Sam says: —You think she had a happy life?

—Happy? Simon says. What's happy? Who says happiness is man's lot? But a full life, yes.

—What's full? Sam says.

—Long, Simon says. On the move. Rich in experience. And then to end up in the care of her loved ones. What more could you ask?

—I never felt she . . . took it in, Sam says. Took in her life, if you know what I mean.

—I know what you mean, Simon says. But is that necessary?

—What?

—To live it and take it in?

—I mean, Sam says. He stops. I don't know quite what I mean, he says.

—I know what you mean, Simon says. But I don't think you're right. Nobody takes their life in but that doesn't mean their life has no meaning. For them or anyone else.

—I'm not saying it should have a religious meaning, Sam says. I just mean . . . You know what I mean.

—I know what you mean, Simon says.

Freddy reads: —'"Wife," said the man, and looked at her. "Are you Pope now?"

'"Yes," she said. "I'm Pope."

'Then he went and stood and looked straight at her, and it was as though he were looking into the bright sun. And when he'd looked at her that way for a long time he said: "How nice for you that you're Pope now."

'But she sat stiff as a poker and didn't move or speak.

'Then he said: "Wife, now please be content. There's nothing more for you to be."

'"I'll think about it," she said. And with that they went to bed.'

—Is it nearly finished? his son asks.

—Nearly. Do you want me to stop?

—No. Go on.

—'The man slept well and soundly,' Freddy read, 'for he'd had an exhausting day. But the woman just couldn't get to sleep, and all night long—'

—Did they burn Nina? Joe asks.

—Yes.

—Completely?

—Yes.

—Why did they do that?

—Because that's what they do when you die.

—Why?

—Why what?

—Why do they do that when you die?

—Because in the old days they buried you when you died and that took up a lot of space. So now there isn't anywhere left to bury people and they burn them instead.

—Because so many people have died?

—And because it's cleaner to burn people.

—It wasn't clean before?

—Not so clean. Do you want me to go on with the story?

—Why is it cleaner to burn than to bury?

—Because fire cleans.

—It doesn't. It makes a mess.
—Not if it's strong enough.
—But if not so many people had died would she have been buried?
—I don't know.
—What happens when you burn?
—Everything is reduced to a few ashes.
—But ashes are dirty.
—They put the ashes in an urn.
—What's a nurn?
—A jar. Shall I go on with the story?
—Why in a jar?
—To give it to the relatives.
—Who did they give it to?
—Granny.
—Granny has it?
—Yes. I think so.
—What's she going to do with it?
—I don't know. You must ask her.
—Is it cleaner in a jar?
—Yes.
—And when there aren't any jars any more?
—There'll always be jars.
—Always?
—For a long time.
—And when I'm dead they'll burn me and put me in a jar?
—Your ashes, yes.
—And who will they give it to?
—To your children.
—And if I don't have any children?
—To your nearest relatives.
—Is that Becky?
—Yes.
—But if Becky's already dead?
—I don't know. They dispose of it as they think best.
—Who do?
—The people who burn the body.
—What people are they?
—Shall I go on or shan't I?
—I'd rather be buried, he says.
—I'm sure that can be arranged.
—You said there wasn't any more room.
—If you insist they find room.

—Then why didn't Gran insist?
—She thought it was cleaner to burn.
—I wouldn't like to be burnt.
—You wouldn't feel anything. You'd be dead. Now will you let me get on with the story?
—No.
—Will you go to sleep then?
—All right.
—You won't be frightened?
—Frightened of what?
—All sorts of things.
—I want to think about Nina.
—All right. You think about her. I'll sit here with you for a while. All right?
—If you want.
—Don't you want me to?
—If you want.
—All right. I'll put out the light and stay here with you and you think about Nina.

*

—My sister thinks so too, Julie says.
—In that case, Licia says.
—I don't know, Julie says.
—If your sister thinks so too.
—What do you think?
—Me?
—It's just not good for the children, Julie says.
—In that case, Licia says.
—On the other hand it's not good for them to have the family break up, is it? Especially after the last few weeks.
—No, Licia says.
—But there does come a point, Julie says.
Licia is silent.
—It isn't as if I haven't tried, Julie says.
—He's been trying too, Licia says.
—It's almost easier to bear when there's someone else, Julie says. You know what I mean?
—Yes, Licia says.
—At least you can blame someone if there's someone else, Julie says. But if there isn't you can only blame yourself.
—Oh no, Licia says.
—And him of course, Julie says.

—Why blame anyone? Licia says. Why not just accept that these things happen?

—Things don't happen by themselves, Julie says. People make them happen.

—Yes, Licia says.

—What have I done? Julie says. Can you tell me what I've done?

—No, Licia says.

—Exactly, Julie says.

Licia is silent.

—Do you think I should? Julie says.

—What?

—See if perhaps . . .

—I thought you said you'd made up your mind, Licia says.

—Yes, Julie says. My sister thinks it would be better.

—I didn't know you paid so much attention to what your sister said, Licia says.

—Who have I got to turn to? Julie says. Especially since Nancy died.

Licia is silent.

—Nancy was someone I could talk everything over with, Julie says.

—Of course, Licia says.

—I'm sorry, Julie says, taking a handkerchief out of her bag and wiping her eyes.

—Where would you go? Licia asks.

—I think he should be the one to go, don't you? Julie says, putting the handkerchief back in her bag.

—I suppose so, Licia says.

—He could come here, couldn't he? Julie says.

—You've discussed this with him?

—No, Julie says.

—He might not want to come back here, Licia says.

—I'm not sure what he wants is relevant, Julie says, sniffing.

—What do you want me to say? Licia says.

—I want you to advise me.

—I can't do that.

—You think it's my fault.

—Did I say that?

—You implied it.

—I did?

—I think so, Julie says. Yes.

—I think it's entirely a matter between you and him, Licia says. You must do what's best for the children. I don't think you should listen to me or your sister.

—She's the only person I have left in the world, Julie says.
Licia is silent.
—At least he can come and talk to you or Ella, Julie says.
—He doesn't.
—At least he can. You've always been close.
—Close doesn't necessarily mean supportive, Licia says.
—You don't know what it's like to have no one, Julie says.
Licia is silent.
—I'm sorry, Julie says. She takes the handkerchief out of her bag and dabs her eyes again.
Licia waits.
—I'm sorry, Julie says again.
She puts the handkerchief away and stands up. Licia stands with her. They walk to the door.
—I thought you'd be able to help, Julie says.
—I'm sorry, Licia says.
—I should have known better, Julie says.
Licia stands, holding the door open.

—A doctor once told me, the man says, that it doesn't matter if one doesn't sleep all night so long as one can stretch out in bed and lie there quietly. What the body needs is rest, he said, the man says. He told me to get up and drink a glass of water if I began to grow restless. It's not much comfort to be told that, the man says, when, after the first half hour in which sleep has almost arrived, you realise you are in for another white night. I'm only saying this, he says, to explain why I keep yawning.

—I hadn't noticed, she says.

—I thought you might take it personally, he says, and laughs.

—I hadn't noticed, she says again.

—Normally, he says, I'm a very sound sleeper.

She is silent.

—Normally, he says, I sleep right through the night without any trouble.

—You're lucky, she says.

—You don't?

—By and large, she says.

—You wake up in the night and read?

—Yes, she says.

—My mother was like that, he says. She did all her reading at night. I can't, he says. I just lie there hoping sleep will come and the more I hope the less it is likely to.

—Do you dream? she asks him.

—Never.

—Never?

—I mean I never remember my dreams. We all dream of course, he adds. It's only a question of whether one remembers one's dreams or not. I don't.

—That's a shame, she says.

—You could say that my days are boring and my nights even more boring, he says.

—It's no fun dreaming, though, she says.

—Why do you say that?

—Why?

She is silent.
Finally he says: —Bereavement does funny things to me.
—Yes, she says.
—I'm sorry, he says.
—Sorry?
—For what you are going through.
—Oh, she says, I'm not sure I'm going through anything.
—I'm still sorry, he says. Though that doesn't help.
She is silent.
—If one didn't worry so much about not being able to go to sleep, he says, one would probably be able to do so without difficulty.
She gets up.
—You have to go? he asks her.
—Yes.
—Your mother is waiting for you?
—I have to go.
—I'll walk with you, he says, getting up too.
—No no, she says. Please.
—It's time I was on my way.
They walk.
—There is another bench there, he says, pointing. I used to sit there.
—What made you change?
—I got tired of that one, he says. I got tired of the view.
—And now?
—Now?
They reach the road.
—I go this way, she says.
He stops.
—Goodbye, she says.
She walks away down the hill.

*

—'The man slept well and soundly,' Freddy reads, 'for he'd had an exhausting day. But the woman just couldn't get to sleep, and all night long she tossed and turned, thinking about what more she could be, but she just couldn't think of anything. As the sun was about to rise, and as she saw the red light of dawn, she sat up in bed and stared straight at it, and when she saw the sun come up, "Aha," she thought, "why couldn't I make the sun and moon rise too?"

'"Husband," she said, and poked him in the ribs with her elbow, "wake up quick. Go to the flounder and tell him I want to be like God."

'The man was still half asleep, but he was so frightened that he fell out of bed. He thought at first he hadn't heard right, and rubbed his eyes and said: "Oh, wife, what are you saying?"

'"Husband," she said, "if I can't make the sun and moon rise, if I can only watch them rise, I just won't be able to bear it. I'll never have an hour of peace again so long as I can't make the sun rise myself." Then she gave him such a terrible look that a shudder went through him: "Go this minute," she said. "Tell the flounder I want to be like God."

'"Oh, wife," said the man, and fell on his knees. "The flounder can't do that. He can make Popes and Emperors – I beg you, think it over and be content with Pope."

'Then she got really angry and her hair flew wildly about her head and she tore her bodice and kicked him, screaming: "I will not stand it any longer! Be off with you!"

'Then he pulled on his trousers and ran off like mad. Outside a storm was raging, so that he could hardly keep his feet. Houses and trees were falling and the mountains shook and the trees rolled into the sea and the sky was pitch black all over and there was thunder and lightning and the sea rose in black waves as high as mountains, topped with crests of white foam. Then he shouted but he . . .'

He stops. He listens to his son's breathing. Then he shuts the book quietly, puts out the light, and creeps out of the room.

In her room his daughter is lying in bed, reading.

He sits down on the bed: —How are you doing?

—I just want to finish this.

—How much more do you have?

—Only a little bit.

He pinches her toes through the blankets. She moves her feet.

—Let me see, he says.

She goes on reading, curled up away from him.

—All right, he says. Finish the story and then put out the light. All right?

—All right.

He kisses her. —Goodnight, he says.

—Goodnight.

He gets up and goes to the door. —Just that story, he says. Promise.

—Promise.

—Goodnight.

—Goodnight.

*

—When you have to pack up and leave a country where you've lived all your life, Nina says, a part of you gets lost, but then something else gets born, so who's to say it isn't a blessing?

—It gets lost for good? Licia asks her.

—It's as if it got mislaid, Nina says. Most of the time you are not even aware of the fact that you've lost it, but then a smell, a sound, is enough to awaken all the old feelings, and then you realise you've lost them for good.

—It was hard to adapt when you came here? Licia finds herself asking.

—Adapting has nothing to do with it, Nina says. Life goes on, wherever one is. But something got mislaid.

—You were sorry to leave? Licia asks her.

—I was thankful to leave, Nina says. I was grateful to fate. Things get lost anyway, she says. As one grows older. All sorts of things. But if one stays in the same place all one's life one is not even aware of it. When you become aware of it you realise that something else has got born.

—Like what? Licia asks.

—Leaving, Nina says, letting go of things, perhaps it's what everyone needs. But it doesn't make it any less painful of course. Or the pang any less violent.

*

—I don't want to talk about it, Julie says.

—I thought you did, her sister says. I thought that's what you wanted.

—No, Julie says. I don't want to talk about it.

—I never did understand you, her sister says.

—Never mind, Julie says.

—Do I take it things are better then? her sister asks.

—No, Julie says.

—Well then, her sister says.

—I don't want to talk about it.

—Suit yourself.

—I will, Julie says.

—You don't look happy, her sister says.

—Who said I was happy?

—Well then, her sister says.

—I just said I didn't want to talk about it.

—Suit yourself, her sister says.

—How do you feel? Ella asks.
—Great, Simon says. Great.
—I'm so glad, Ella says.
—Just every now and again around the heart, Simon says.
—How do you mean, around the heart?
—Just a sort of dull pain.
—You don't think you should see a doctor?
—What will a doctor do? Simon says. I'm an old man. That sort of thing's natural at my age.
—He might give you something to take.
—To make me young again?
—To relieve the pain.
—And then what? Simon says. It'll just break out elsewhere.
—Elsewhere where?
—I told you, Simon says. All in all everything's great.
—But you said your heart.
—At least I know I'm alive, Simon says. If you're hurting you can't be dead, can you?
—I wish you wouldn't talk like that, Ella says.
—You asked.
—I wanted to know how you were.
—I told you, Simon says. Great. Except now and again this pain round the heart.
—I think you should see a doctor, Ella says.
—When did a doctor ever do me any good?
—You're afraid they'll put you back in hospital, Ella says.
—Of course I'm afraid.
—It's for your own good.
—They almost killed me, Simon says. You want them to finish the job off now?
—Don't talk like that, Ella says.
—I told you, Simon says. I'm in great shape. What's a little pain round the heart now and again?
—Don't joke about these things, Ella says. Health is too serious to joke about.

—Nothing's too serious to joke about, Simon says. That's what you've never understood, Ella. Just like your father. Nothing's too serious to joke about.

*

—She seemed to be bearing up very well, Robin says.
—Bearing up? Freddy says.
—All things considered, Robin says.
—How do you mean exactly, all things considered?
—Well with your grandmother's death and all that, Robin says.
—It wasn't exactly unexpected, Freddy says.
—It wasn't?
—It's not like someone suddenly snuffing out at fifty, Freddy says.
—Even so, Robin says.
—She died in her sleep, Freddy says. What better death can there be than that?
—And you? Robin says.
—What about me?
—Has it affected you?
—Of course it's bloody well affected me, Freddy says.
—I'm sorry, Robin says. I didn't mean —
—It doesn't matter, Freddy says.
—I wanted to offer my sincere condolences, Robin says.
—Of course, Freddy says.
—I hope she didn't think it was intrusive, Robin says.
—Intrusive? Freddy says. To express your condolences?
—You know what I mean, Robin says.
—I'm sure she was touched, Freddy says.
—She told you so?
—No. But I'm sure she was.
—I'm glad, Robin says. I was afraid I was intruding.
—What do you think of this then? Nigel asks as he slides up to them.
—So-so.
—It's an idea.
—Nineteen thirteen, nineteen thirty-nine, Nigel says. It has quite a good ring to it.
—So has seventeen eighty-eight, nineteen sixteen, Freddy says.
—Why not? Nigel says.
—I feel Charley missed an opportunity.
—It's too thin. There's no Austrian stuff for one thing.
—That's because of the Maastricht show.
—Then why not wait a year?

—You'll tell her how sorry I am? Robin says.
—Because then they'll have to wait six.
—I don't get it.
—I thought you told her yourself? Freddy says.
—Three. Nine.
—You're not persuading me.
—But I'd like you to tell her too, Robin says.
—Have you been to the Maastricht show?
—I did an interview with Bo.
—Who for?
—You won't forget?
—No, Freddy says.
—Do you think it would be a good idea if I looked in one of these days?
—Looked in? On me?
—No. On Liss.
—How should I know?
—Did he tell you about Kokoschka and his mother?
—His own mother?
—Who else's?
—I thought you might mean Kokoschka's.
—No no. His own.
—I don't think so.
—It's quite a story.
—Do you think I should ring first? Robin asks. Just to make sure she's in?
—Not just Kokoschka, of course. Alban Berg.
—Alban Berg?
—He didn't tell you?
—Do you? I don't want her to feel I'm intruding.
—Perhaps you'd better.
—I thought as I had to pass that way when I called on my godmother I . . .
—I knew about his mother and Max Ernst. But Alban Berg . . .!
—You'll have to get him to tell you.
—I certainly will!

*

—Forgive me, the man says. I should have offered you one.
—No thank you, Licia says.
—They're not very nice, the man says. He holds the open box out to her.
—No thank you, she says again.

—It's the time of year for sore throats, the man says.
—Yes, Licia says.
—It always begins with my throat, the man says. Forgive me, he says again. My breath stinks.
—Oh . . . Licia says.
—One doesn't know what to wear, the man says.
—I know, Licia says.
—Soon, he says, it will be too cold to sit.
She is silent.
—Soon only the walkers with their dogs will be about, he says.
—You don't come here in the winter? she asks.
—And the walkers without their dogs, he says. Hoods up, hands stuffed into their pockets.
—Yes, she says.
—People sometimes try to calculate how many hours a human being spends sleeping in the course of a lifetime, he says. But it would be equally interesting to try to work out how many miles they walk and how many words they utter. On average.
She is silent.
—It would cast an unexpected light on the species, I suspect, he says.
She is silent.
—One might be able to calculate how often certain words are used in an average lifetime, he says.
—They would have to be recorded, she says.
—It isn't difficult to imagine them being recorded somewhere, he says.
—I know, she says.
—Oh? he says.
—I imagine that too sometimes, she says. From the first to the last.
He takes the box out of his pocket again and offers it to her.
—No thank you, she says.
He takes a lozenge, puts it in his mouth, shuts the box, puts it back in his pocket.
—From the first to the last, he repeats.
—Yes, she says.
—If they are not recorded somewhere then where *do* they go? he says. They fade into the air.
—Perhaps somebody remembers them, she says.
—And then that somebody too is forgotten, he says. They too fade into the air.
—Yes, she says.

He is silent.
She looks at her watch.
—Time to go? he says.
—Yes.
She gets up. He rises with her.
They begin to walk.
He takes the box out of his pocket again, offers it to her.
—No thank you, she says.
He takes a lozenge, puts it in his mouth, returns the box to his pocket.
They walk away from the Common.
—Here we are, she says.
—Here we are.
—Goodbye.
—Remember, he says, someone, somewhere is recording them.
—Or not, she says.
—Or not, he agrees.

—Where do you want to start? Freddy asks his daughter.
—You show me, she says.
—We'll start with William Blake. Do you remember William Blake?
—Yes.
—Are you happy to start there?
—Yes.
—We'll ignore these rooms. They're full of terrible pictures.
—Why terrible?
—I find them terrible. When you're old enough to come by yourself you can look at them and make up your own mind. Not with me.
—Who painted them?
—Some terrible painters called Pre-Raphaelites.
—Preera . . .?
—They wanted to go back to before Raphael.
—Why?
—You remember Raphael? We saw some of his pictures in the Victoria and Albert Museum.
—Those big ones?
—Yes. Very big.
—Why did they want to go back to before him?
—They thought painting was better then. They were quite right. But it didn't help their own work. Now look. Here are the Blakes. Do you remember them?
—Yes.
—Look at them carefully. Which do you prefer?
—I like that little one of the sheep.
—Why?
—I like the moonlight.
—I like it too. It's not by Blake though. It's by another great English painter, Samuel Palmer. Here's another one by him.
—Was he at the same time as Blake?
—He was a disciple of Blake's. He was a young man when Blake was already very old. He and his friends worshipped Blake.

—I like that one best.
—I agree with you. Why?
– I don't like the way Blake does his people.
—Do you like any of them?
—Is that one by Blake?
—Yes.
—I like it.
—What do you like about it?
—I don't know. I like his beard. And his colour.
—Nearly all Blake's paintings are illustrations of his poems. And the poems are comments on the pictures. He was the only artist since the Middle Ages who felt pictures and words went completely together. Do you know any poems by Blake?
—Do I?
—Yes you do.
—What?
—Tyger tyger burning bright.
—In the forests of the night.
—Go on.
—I can't. You go on.
—What immortal hand or eye Framed thy fearful symmetry.
—Can we have a cup of chocolate?
—Why not? Then we can go and see the Turners.
—What about the woodpeckers?
—What woodpeckers?
—You said you'd show me the woodpeckers and the mirrors.
—Oh. Yes. Rebecca Horn. Let's go and see her before we have our chocolate. Right?
—Right.
—Come on. We'll hurry past this stuff. Nobody can look at more than ten works of art in any one session.
—Nobody?
—Well they can of course but they won't look at them properly.
—Where's Rebecca Horn?
—We're getting there. It's a big gallery.
—Has she got a horn?
—No. She's German.
—Germans don't have horns?
—No.
—Only the English?
—Yes.
—Where's your horn then?
—I'm not English.

—What are you?
—I don't know. Not English.
—Am I English?
—A bit more than me.
—And my children? Will they be English?
—Probably a little more than you.
—And their children?
—A little more each time.
—Until they're completely English?
—No one is completely anything. Here we are. Close your eyes and give me your hand. Do you hear the woodpeckers?
—Yes.
—Just hold my hand and step forward.
—Are they real woodpeckers?
—You'll see.
—Can I open my eyes now?
—Yes. Don't move. Do you see us reflected in that mirror at the end?
—Yes.
—Turn round. Do you see us reflected for ever in those other mirrors?
—Are those the woodpeckers?
—Yes.
—They're not real.
—No. Listen. They all peck at different speeds and make slightly different noises as their beaks touch the glass: Poom! Silence. Poom! Silence. Poom-poom! Silence. Poom po-poom. Silence —poom!
—There's a different one here.
—Yes. Look. It's plunging its beak into a bunch of charcoal sticks. Look. Each time the beak goes in it makes a different noise from the others and each time a little bit of charcoal dust floats down onto that great white egg below.
—Why is it there?
—You'll have to ask her.
—Is she here?
—I mean your guess is as good as mine.
—And what's that on the floor in front of those mirrors?
—It's a container full of mercury. You know mercury? Like they have in thermometers.
—Why?
—I don't know that either. Perhaps she feels it's the opposite to the violence of the beaks and to the reflecting power of the mirrors. It's very still and very opaque.

—Do the beaks go on hitting the mirrors all the time?
—Yes.
—Why don't they break them?
—I suspect they stop just short of them.
—They go on even at night?
—I don't know. Perhaps they switch the current off at night. Do you like it?
—It's frightening.
—Yes.
—I don't like it.
—Sometimes with art one likes and one doesn't like at the same time. Sometimes one is frightened but one feels it's better to be frightened than not to have any response at all.
—Can we have our chocolate now?
—Yes. Are you disappointed?
—No. I'm glad we came.
—So am I. Let's have our chocolate and then if we feel like it we can come back and look at some of the Turners.

—Do you want to see the tree? Nina says.
—Oh yes please! Licia says.
—Then follow me.
In her room she throws open the window and stands back:
—There!
Licia stands beside her and together they look out and down at the flowering laburnum.
—What do you think of it?
—It's wonderful.
—Didn't I tell you it was better from here?
—Yes you did.
—It's even better than it was last year, isn't it?
—Much better.
—Feast your eyes, Nina says. Feast your eyes. I'm going to lie down.
After a while she says: —When you've finished sit down at the foot of the bed and tell me what you've been doing.
—Feast your eyes first, she repeats, then sit down and tell me what you've been doing.

*

—Have you told him?
—Not yet, Julie says.
—And you know the children will want to come with you? her sister asks.
—They're not staying with him.
—That's not what I asked.
—What are you trying to do? Julie says. Undermine my confidence?
—I want you to see things as they are, her sister says.
—And you know better than I do how they are?
—I'm less involved, her sister says.
—I'm sorry, Julie says.
—It may feel good for a moment, her sister says, but life's made up of an awful lot of moments.

—I've made up my mind, Julie says.
—If you haven't told him nothing's settled, her sister says.
—I've made up my mind.
—That's not the point.
—It's easy for them to like him, Julie says. He doesn't have them on his hands all day. He can come in in the evening and read to them or take them out to a museum once in a while and he thinks he's being a wonderful father.
—I'm not asking you that, her sister says. I'm asking whether they will want to come with you if you split up.
—They're not staying with him, Julie says.
—You're not being rational, her sister says.
—Would you be rational in my place?
—I'm only trying to help, her sister says.
—I'm sorry, Julie says.
—I don't want you to do anything you'll regret, her sister says.
—I regret every moment I'm still with him, Julie says.
—You've thought of the harm it might do them?
—What about now? Julie says. You don't think it's doing them harm?
—From what I've seen of them they don't seem to be aware of anything unusual, her sister says.
—You know what children are like.
—One can usually see it.
—They're holding it down. They don't know themselves.
—How do you know?
—I know.
—They won't talk to you about it?
—You know what children are like, Julie says. They hold these things down. They don't talk. They don't admit it to themselves. But it doesn't mean they aren't aware of it.
—That's not my experience of children, her sister says.
—Well it's mine, Julie says.
—I only wanted to help, her sister says.
—I know, Julie says. I'm sorry.

*

—It's a nice room, Simon says.
—It's the nicest room in the house, Ella says.
—That's what I'm saying.
—It always was, Ella says.
—That's what I'm saying, Simon says again.
—But it's hers, Ella says. It can't ever be anything but hers.
—You're being sentimental, Ella, Simon says.

—I've tried, Ella says. I've gone up there and sat in the chair and tried to imagine it as something else. But I can't.
—Of course you can't, he says. But if it becomes something else you'd soon get used to it. Like new roads.
—I can't.
—It would save me rent, Simon says.
—I can't, Ella says again.
—It would save Sam the trouble of driving all the way out to fetch me on Sundays.
—No, Simon, Ella says. I'm sorry.
—It was just a thought, Simon says. I like my independence too you know.
—I know, she says.
—It's only after what happened I get scared sometimes. I get the feeling I'm going to fall over.
—It'll pass, Ella says.
—I thought so, you know, Simon says. But it seems to be getting worse.
—I'm sorry, Ella says.
—I know how it is, Simon says. It just seems a terrible waste.
—I've suggested to Liss that she move in there, Ella says. But she can't either.
—She wants to go on living at home?
—She hasn't said she doesn't.
—It was only a thought, Simon says.
—If she did you could have her room.
—I wouldn't want to be living in the midst of you, Simon says.
—No, I can see that, Ella says. But I thought it only fair to ask her first. But she can't either.
—My independence means a great deal to me, as you know, Simon says.
—I know, Ella says.
—Up there, Simon says, I wouldn't be in your way and you wouldn't be in mine. We wouldn't need to see each other all day if we didn't want.
—I'm sorry, Ella says.
—I just thought it would save Sam the trouble of coming all the way out to pick me up and then carting me all the way back.
—It's no trouble, Ella says. He enjoys it.
—I think he enjoys it too, Simon says. It gives us a chance to have a chat.
—He doesn't know what to do with his time, these days, Ella says.

—And I'm not going to be around much longer, Simon says.
—Don't talk like that, Ella says.
—We've got to face the facts, haven't we? Simon says.
—I don't like it when you talk like that.
—It was just a thought, Simon says. It would have meant sacrificing my independence, to a large extent.
—I thought you treasured your independence, Ella says.
—I do, Simon says. That's what I'm saying. I do treasure it. But I hate to see waste. I hate to see good money going down the drain.
—It's not waste, Ella says. It's still her room.
—If I were you, Simon says, I wouldn't think in those terms. It's not good for you.
—I know, Ella says. But I can't help it.
—It was just a thought, Simon says.
—I know, Ella says. I'm sorry.

—Nanny never went out without a razor blade and a bottle of iodine, Nina says. Mummy was terrified that we would be stung by a scorpion.

—Were there many scorpions in Egypt?

—In the desert, yes. Nanny was supposed to cut out the stung part and pour in the iodine as soon as it happened.

—Did it ever happen?

—Thank goodness, no, Nina says. But you had to be prepared. If you were stung there wasn't time to go back for a doctor.

—And she would have known how to do it?

—Oh yes, Nina says. She'd done it once when one of her former charges was stung.

—How terrible, Licia says.

—We didn't think of it like that, Nina says. We felt we were safe with her.

—And the child survived?

—Oh yes, Nina says. Nanny knew how to do those things.

—Did you ever see a scorpion? Licia asks.

—Not in the desert, Nina says. We saw a man with scorpions once. He was showing them off.

—He wasn't afraid of being stung?

—It was very frightening, Nina says. We watched with the rest of the crowd.

—Perhaps he'd removed the sting.

—He probably had, Nina says. But we didn't think of that at the time. We were terrified.

—I'm not surprised, Licia says.

*

—Where is she? Sam asks.

—In Nina's room, his wife says.

—You've spoken to her?

—What do you mean, spoken to her? Ella says.

—I asked you to speak to her.

—I told you I couldn't.
—What's she doing?
—Sitting.
—Just sitting?
—Yes.
—And she's going to spend the rest of her life doing that?
—I don't know, she says.
—That's what she's going to do, he says. She's going to spend the rest of her life here, sitting. And you're not going to do anything about it.
—What can I do?
—After all the education we've given her, he says. And all she does is sit.
—Give her a chance, she says.
—A chance? he says. What do you mean, a chance?
She is silent.
—Haven't we given her a chance? he says. Haven't we given her every chance in the world? And has that changed anything?
—Please, she says.
—At least if she was ill, he says. But all she is is tired. Well I'm tired of her being tired, do you understand?
—Yes, she says.
—How many more chances does she need? he says.
—She has to think things through, she says.
—What? he says. What has she got to think through?
—She has to make sure any decision she takes is the right one.
—Decision? he says. When's the last time she made a decision? And she won't even talk to me any more, he says.
—You frighten her.
—Me? he says. You must be joking.
—You shout at her. It frightens her.
—She frightens me, he says. Sitting there.
—It'll be all right, she says.
—What will?
—Everything.
—You think it'll be all right?
—She needs time, she says.
—How much time?
—I don't know how much time. She needs to feel we're supporting her.
—Why won't she talk to me any more? he says. I'm her father, aren't I?
—You frighten her, she says. You shout and it frightens her.

—I'd understand if the doctors could find something wrong with her, she says.

—She's tired, she says.

—What's she done to get tired? he says. She spends all day sitting. How can she be tired?

—I don't know, she says.

—Why isn't she interested in anything any more? he says. She was always interested in things. Both children were.

—I don't know, she says.

—Jews have always been interested in things, he says. That's why they've always been good at things. What's this attitude all of a sudden? Is it our fault?

—No, dear, she says.

—Then it's her fault.

—Why does it have to be anybody's fault?

—Is it this country's fault?

—Why does it have to be anybody's fault?

—Nobody's interested in things any more, he says. No wonder everybody's tired.

—We just need to be patient, she says. It'll pass, like everything else.

—Is it passing? he says. Does it show any sign of passing? On the contrary. It just grows worse and worse. Now she won't even talk to me any more.

She is silent.

—She's just sitting? he says. She's not doing anything?

—I don't know, she says.

—Well you've been up to see her.

She is silent.

—At least she would answer back, he says. At least she used to quarrel with me. Now she doesn't even answer.

—You frighten her, she says.

—I only want to do what's good for her.

—I know, she says.

—It drives me mad, he says.

—Don't, she says.

—Don't what?

—Don't get into a state about it, she says. Give her time.

—How much time?

—Just time. You're not giving it to her if you're always counting it.

—I haven't given her time? he asks.

—Not if you go on at her like that.

—I don't go on at her, he says. She doesn't speak to me. How can I go on at her if she doesn't respond?
—Well, let her be.
—For how long? For how long do you want me to let her be?
—Just let her be, she says. It doesn't hurt you to have her here.
—It hurts me to see her doing nothing, he says. With her gifts and qualifications. Doing nothing.
—It'll come, she says. Just give it time.

*

—'And the sky was pitch black all over,' Freddy reads, 'and there was thunder and lightning and the sea came in black waves as high as mountains, topped with crests of white foam. Then he shouted but he couldn't hear his own words:

> "Munntje munntje timper tee
> Flounder, flounder in the sea –
> My good wife, dame Ilsebill,
> Wills not what I'd have her will."

'"Well, what does she want this time?" said the flounder.
'"Ah, flounder," said the man, "she wants to be like God."
'"Just go on home, she's back in the stinking hovel again."
'And they're sitting there to this very day.'

—Hold up your two fingers like this, Simon says.
—Like this?
—Then I pass the string round this finger, Simon says, and then this finger, and now watch carefully, I move my hand round like this, I hold the string here and here, and then I put my fingers down on top of yours. All right?
—All right, Becky says.
—There isn't a gap between the tips of our fingers?
—No.
—Now watch carefully. Hey presto and away comes the string!
—Do it again, Becky says.
—All right. Hold your two fingers up like this. I'll do it very slowly this time. First I pass the string round this finger and then I pass it round that one. All right?
—All right.
—I thought I'd put twice the amount of fertiliser, Sam says, and give them twice as much water. All the books warned against but I was right, wasn't I?
—I've never seen so many, Julie says.
—Sweet, Sam says. So sweet you'd think you were eating a peach, not a common or garden tomato. How many do you want?
—Whatever you can spare.
—There's no shortage, as you can see, Sam says.
—She doesn't speak to him any more, Ella says.
—What do you mean? Freddy says.
—She just doesn't take the trouble to reply.
—How does he react?
—It's driving him mad.
—He doesn't look any madder than usual.
—You know what I mean, she says.
—I'm not surprised, Freddy says. Not after the way he goes on at her.
—Won't you talk to her? his mother says.
—Talk to her?
—She'd listen to you. You're the only one she'll listen to.

—What am I supposed to tell her?
—You know what I mean.
—There's a man at the door, Joe says.
—A man? What does he want?
—I don't know.
—Didn't you ask him?
—I don't know.
—I'll go and see, Ella says.
—Now you do it, Simon says.
—I can't, Becky says.
—Go on. I'll show you how. I hold up my hand like that. Right? Now you pass the string round one finger and then round the other. Right?
—And then?
—Then you take hold of it like this. Hold on. It's difficult to do on oneself. Hold on. No. Go back one. All right. You pass it round the two fingers, then you take it like that, gently, gently, and turn over like that. Now you pause and make sure there isn't a gap between the tips of the fingers, then, hey presto, and off it comes!
—Let me try again.
Ella comes back. —He wants Liss, she says.
—Who is it?
—I don't know.
—What does he want?
—He says he was passing and thought he'd look in.
—And you don't know who it is?
—Go and talk to him, she says.
Freddy goes to the door.
—I didn't mean to intrude, the man says. I was just passing and thought I'd call in and see how she was.
—Who are you?
—A friend.
—Oh?
—We met on the Common.
—She's fine, Freddy says.
—Is she about?
—I'll see. Won't you come in?
—I'll wait here, the man says. I don't want to intrude.
—You're not intruding, Freddy says. Come into the hall at least.
—I haven't seen her for a while, the man says, stepping in. I hoped she was all right.
—I'll have a look, Freddy says.
He goes back in. —Where is she? he asks his mother.

—Who is it?
—A man she met on the Common.
—She's never mentioned him.
—Where is she?
—Try her room. Or Nina's.
—Nina's?
—She sits there a lot nowadays.

He climbs the stairs. He calls her name. On the landing he turns left. He knocks at the door of her room but there is no reply. He opens the door and surveys the empty room.

He closes the door and returns to the stairs. He climbs up to the second floor. The door is open. He goes in.

—There's a man for you, he says.
—Oh?
—He says you met on the Common.
—What does he want?
—He wants to talk to you.
—I don't know him.
—You don't know him? How does he know your name? Where you live?
—What's he look like?
—Tall. With an anorak.
—I don't know him.
—You don't know any tall men with anoraks.
—No.
—He wants to talk to you.
—I don't know him, she says. Tell him to go away.
—Are you coming down for lunch?
—Is it ready?
—No. I just wondered.
—I don't know the time.
—Don't you have a watch?
—It's stopped.
—You won't speak to this man?
—What does he want?
—He didn't say. He said he was passing and hadn't seen you for some time and wondered how you were.
—Tell him I don't live here any more.
—I can't do that.
—Tell him you don't know where I am.
—All right, he says. If that's what you want.

He goes down. —I can't find her, he says to the man. I'm sorry. Was it urgent?

—No no, the man says. I was just passing and thought I'd look in.
—You want to leave a message?
—Just tell her I called.
—Who do I say?
—It doesn't matter, the man says. I'm sorry I disturbed you.
—So what do I tell her?
—It doesn't matter.
—Suit yourself, Freddy says.

The man turns away. Freddy closes the front door behind him. He goes into the kitchen. His mother is sitting at the table and crying. He puts his arms round her.

—I'm sorry, she says. I'm sorry.
—It's all right.
—It takes me like that sometimes, she says. I'll be all right in a minute.

His son tugs at his trousers: —Can I have a chocolate, Dad?
—Not before lunch.
—I'm hungry.
—We'll eat soon.
—Why is Granny crying?
—She's thinking of Nina.
—Can't I have just one?
—No. Leave us alone, there's a good boy.
—When will we eat?
—When it's ready. Now get out.
—I'll pick them for you after lunch, Sam says.
—You won't forget?
—Do I forget?
—No, Julie says.
—You'll see, he says. Sweeter than peaches.
—Try it once more, Simon says.
—No, Becky says. I'm tired.
—Do you want me to show you another one?
—No. When are we going to eat?
—Any minute now.
—I'm hungry.
—So am I. Listen to my tummy. Can you hear it gurgle?
—I'll go and see if I can help Granny, Becky says.
—Listen, Simon says, holding up his hand. Can you hear it gurgle?